The Mystery of Grimly Manor

The Mystery of Grimly Manor

Donna Wren Carson

BOOKSIDE Press

Copyright © 2024 by Donna Wren Carson

ISBN: 978-1-77883-452-3 (Paperback)

All rights reserved. No part of this publication may be reproduced, distributed, or transmitted in any form or by any means, including photocopying, recording, or other electronic or mechanical methods, without the prior written permission of the publisher, except in the case brief quotations embodied in critical reviews and other noncommercial uses permitted by copyright law.

The views expressed in this book are solely those of the author and do not necessarily reflect the views of the publisher, and the publisher hereby disclaims any responsibility for them.

BOOKSIDE Press

BookSide Press
877-741-8091
www.booksidepress.com
orders@booksidepress.com

Dedicated to: Susan Carson
In memory of Arlington Armstrong

Contents

Prologue ix

Chapter 1	Moving Day 1
Chapter 2	Another New Friend? 5
Chapter 3	Super Sunday 10
Chapter 4	Grimly Manor 13
Chapter 5	The First Day of School! 17
Chapter 6	A Knock on the Door 22
Chapter 7	Buttering Up Our Parents! 27
Chapter 8	A Light in the Cemetery 31
Chapter 9	Weekend Woes and Monday Nightmares! 36
Chapter 10	Discovery in the Cemetery 41
Chapter 11	The Thirtieth of October 47
Chapter 12	Halloween! 53
Chapter 13	A Birthday Present 58
Chapter 14	A Campout 63
Chapter 15	A Long but Memorable Week 69
Chapter 16	Thanksgiving 74
Chapter 17	Caroling 80
Chapter 18	Snowed In 86
Chapter 19	Christmas Surprise! 92
Chapter 20	A Grimly Ending 100

Prologue

SHE CREPT SLOWLY toward the foreboding manor. The stench of wet decaying leaves wafting upward filled her senses with dread. Through the darkness, she could see the flickering of one lone candle through a cracked, grimy window. Never before had she found the courage to come so far. Sweat poured from her brows even as a chill wind swept by. She was almost at the window now. Soon—very soon—she would discover if the reclusive owner of Grimly Manor was exhuming corpses from the graveyard behind it. As she slowly lifted her head to peer through the window, an ear-piercing shriek shattered the night's silence, and she watched in horror as a wolf of unbelievable size came charging toward the window! The glass shattered and with its jaws opened wide…

The realization hit me that I was the girl!

Suddenly, my mother jarred me awake from my worst nightmare yet. Groggily, but with my heart hammering, my mom sympathetically asked, "Did you have another scary dream about the old Grimly Manor down the road?" I nodded as I tried to shake off the effects of the dream. How would I ever get over my fear of the decrepit manor and the cemetery surrounding it?

Chapter 1
Moving Day

SEVERAL DAYS LATER, after breakfast, I curled up in my comfy chair, gazing out the living room window. I saw Pickles, my grumpy neighbor's dog, running exuberantly toward a woman pushing her baby down the street in a stroller. After a quick phone call from my mom, the dog responded immediately to her owner's grouchy shout. Actually, Pickles was a beautiful, friendly Labrador retriever, but he could be a little overenthusiastic at times. I'm not sure exactly why Mrs. Numarker named her dog Pickles, but I can guess that it was to reflect her own sour disposition. Anyway, my mother ended up saving the day for the mother, even if Mrs. Numarker didn't appreciate it! Other than that one event, the summer had been extremely boring.

Today, the thirtieth of August, something exciting was finally happening! New people were moving in to the house next door to mine, and later in the week, another family would be moving into the neighborhood. The house next to mine was a light green two-story home with a two-car garage. The only disgusting thing about it was that the previous owners had painted the shutters fluorescent lime green! The other house that sold was directly across the street. Besides the dreaded Grimly Manor, it was the most impressive house in the neighborhood. The previous owners had added a third-floor turreted room to it that was totally awesome! There was also a large garage with a studio built above it. I think one of the former owners was an artist. It had wood shingles painted antique blue with ivory shutters. A white picket fence surrounded the yard. I would love to check out the inside someday. I still couldn't figure out why no one had bought the place until now.

Anyway, I was hoping with all my heart that one of the new families had a daughter my age. In eleven years, all I'd come across are crotchety old folks or young couples with new babies in our neighborhood. There are a few older boys around, but they were mostly troublemakers. What I wanted most was a special friend to share adventures with and confide in. Occasionally, my parents allowed me to have a friend from school or Irish step dancing over, but that definitely didn't happen very often.

Just then, some vehicles turning to our street captured my attention. I thought excitedly, *It's a moving van.* A large truck and two cars were following it around the corner! They passed my house and stopped at the house next door. It was finally happening—and I was soooo nervous. One vehicle was a small slightly rusty white car, and the other was a new black minivan. As they slowed down and pulled into the driveway, I strained to see who was inside the minivan. Unfortunately, I couldn't tell because of the dark-tinted windows. I waited impatiently for the minivan door to slide open. Out stepped a somewhat slim young woman with a small girl—disappointedly, the girl looked to be about six or seven years old. But then I noticed another girl emerging out from the other side. She looked slightly older than me, but my mom had repeatedly said I'm petite, so I thought maybe she could be my age. I truly hoped so!

With anticipation suddenly pulsing through my veins, I jumped up from the chair and started practicing my Irish step dancing. It was the only thing I could do to let out the energy that quickly had built up inside me. I danced for several minutes until I had settled my nerves enough and then plunked down into the chair to watch my new neighbors start moving in.

As I continued to watch them unload, I nervously thought to myself, *What should I say to her?* I was actually very shy with new people. So I practiced aloud by saying, "Hi, my name is Leira Jean MacGregor, and I'm an only child. I'm starting sixth grade this year. I can't wait because this will be my last year of elementary school." At that point, I stopped, grimaced, and thought, *Maybe I should just introduce myself. I definitely don't want to sound like an idiot.*

Excitedly, I hoped this might be the best friend I've been waiting for! She might even be someone who has enough nerve to go near Grimly Manor with me.

Grimly Manor was an old decrepit mansion at the end of our street, with an even older graveyard partially surrounding it. It was the only place in the neighborhood that wasn't new, like the rest. It was totally creepy not only because of the way it looked, but strange things happened there that never got explained—except with rumors. I had always been too afraid to get too close to it by myself because of what I had heard. Every once in a while, I had the same reoccurring nightmare about it, and even though I loved mysteries, especially if they were a bit eerie, I definitely couldn't go there alone. But... if I had someone fearless enough to investigate it with, then maybe I could uncover the mysterious things that went on there, and my nightmares would go away. Hopefully, one of my new neighbors would be someone with enough courage to face the challenge with me!

Thoughts of Grimly Manor and frightening nightmares vanished from my mind as I glanced out the window again. Much to my joy, the older girl next door was outside, walking along the bushes that separated our yards. Her hand was lightly grazing the tips of the shrubs. Intrigued, I thought, *She's singing.* Instantly, I leapt up, ran out the door, and then hesitantly walked up to the bushes between our houses.

Nervously, I said, "Hi, my name is Leira Jean MacGregor, and I'm eleven years old. I'm starting sixth grade next week at J. P. Gooding Elementary School. Welcome to our neighborhood."

She looked at me with an enormous sincere smile. As she extended her hand, a swift breeze blew her medium length, extremely dark brown hair across her face, and while pushing it back, she replied, laughing a bit, "Hi! I'm Adriana Marie Davies and not only am I eleven too, but I'm also starting sixth grade! My friends call me Addy. I guess we're going to the same school. Isn't that fantastic? Maybe, we'll even be in the same classroom!"

I felt an immediate bond between us. I was so excited that she was my age and also very friendly. I had noticed earlier that she had a younger sister, so I asked about her.

Addy replied, "Oh. That's my little sister Josie. She can be a real pain because she constantly wants to tag along after me. Other times she's all right, but mostly she'll drive you crazy. I think it's because I'm older than she is. You'll understand what I mean after you've known her for a while. She's only seven and is starting second grade."

I said, "Next year we'll both be starting middle school, and I'm kind of nervous, or to be honest, scared to death of junior high! That will be an adventure in itself."

Addy replied, "I feel the same way. My mom keeps telling me, 'Don't worry about that yet. Good grief, you haven't even started sixth grade yet!'"

I laughed and said, "That's exactly what my mom says. Both of my parents work, although they still make as much time as possible to spend with me—or grump at me! My dad is an engineer that works on parts that go into airplanes. Somehow, that makes me feel better when I fly out to Arizona to visit my aunt Debbie."

Addy asked in amazement, "Your aunt lives in Arizona and you've flown there?"

I replied, "Yeah, I've been there three or four times. Hey! Maybe sometime you could come with us!"

Addy replied optimistically, "Well, maybe if our parents become friends, then who knows? That would be totally awesome!"

At that moment, Addy's mother called to her, saying that she needed to come back and help unpack. Addy yelled over shoulder, "I'll be there in a minute, Mom. I'm just making a new friend." Glancing back at me, Addy said, "Sorry, but I've got to go now. Hopefully we can get together tomorrow."

As Addy turned to go, I quickly replied, "I hope so too!" Then, as she was walking away, I shouted out, "Wait!"

Addy paused and turned around, and I said, "I just wanted to tell you that there's another family moving in across the street, this week, I think. Maybe they'll have someone we can be friends with too. That house," I said, pointing across the street, "has been for sale for a really long time, but I don't know why. It's so beautiful."

As Addy was about to say something, her mother shouted, "Adriana Marie Davies! You get over here this instant and help us unpack!"

Addy quickly hurried away as she yelled back over her shoulder, "See you soon, Leira!"

Chapter 2
Another New Friend?

EVEN THOUGH WE didn't get to spend too much time together, Addy and I became close friends during the week she moved in.

On the following Saturday morning, I awoke unusually early, remembering this would be the first day I would be able to spend the whole afternoon with Addy.

The morning dragged on forever, but we finally got together after lunch. We spent seemingly endless hours talking about our dreams and fears, including starting sixth grade on Monday. Addy reminded me to tell her about an adventure I had mentioned the first day we met, about my favorite Beanie Baby, Nippy.

I said, "OK. When I was about six years old, I lost my favorite Beanie, Nippy."

Addy interrupted and asked, "What does she look like? We haven't compared our collections yet, and I don't have one named Nippy."

I replied, "Well, she's a kitty, who's mostly brown with ivory spots. Anyway, I had two others exactly like her, but to me they weren't the 'real' Nippy. I cried and cried. My mom, dad, nana, and grandpa searched everywhere. And even though my mother gave me one of the other Nippies I had, it just wasn't the same. She was too new. I called her Nippy Number Two. Then, you won't believe what happened!" Addy looked at me expectantly. I said, "Just a few weeks later, I lost Nippy Number Two."

Addy exclaimed, "That's awful!"

I nodded and continued. "After a few days of searching, my mom gave me my last Nippy. Of course, I called her Nippy Number Three. I had her for about eight months when my grandpa called one day and asked happily, 'Guess who I found in the spare bedroom closet?'

"I screamed, 'Nippy?'

"My grandpa laughed and said, 'I'll be right over!'

"I was so incredibly happy, you wouldn't believe it! Unfortunately, when he arrived and handed her to me, I took one glance and knew it wasn't Nippy Number One. It turned out to be Nippy Number Two."

I hesitated for a moment and then asked Addy, "Are you confused yet?"

With an enormous smile, she gasped, "No! Just tell me what happened next!"

Grinning, I continued, "Well, I was disappointed, but I tried not to let my grandpa know. But the story doesn't end there. About half a year later while Grandpa was raking leaves, he was cleaning off the bushes and was completely amazed to find my original Nippy stuck down inside them. She'd been there for way over a year! Can you believe it?"

Addy replied, "No way! That's incredible!" Quickly she asked, "Can you go get them and show them to me?"

I raced upstairs, and within a few moments, I hurried back down carrying all three of my Nippies. While Addy was looking at each one, she questioned me about them, and after I answered all her questions, she abruptly changed the subject by asking, "What's up with that creepy old place at the end of the street with the cemetery around it?"

Glancing away from her, I licked my dry lips and tried to hide my fear as I replied, "That's the old Grimly place. They say old Albert Grimly lives there now, but no one knows very much about him. There are a bunch of rumors about him and the manor, but I think it's best if I don't say anymore for now."

Addy looked extremely nervous, but slightly curious as she asked, "Is there some reason why you can't tell me anything more right now? I feel scared because I get the feeling that you're frightened to tell me more."

I answered honestly, "Well… the only reason I can give you right now is that I'm not sure if it's the right time to talk about it." I looked into her eyes and said, "Just trust me—for now."

At the look of confusion in Addy's eyes, I continued reassuringly, "Don't worry. It's not as bad as it sounds. I'd just feel better talking about it another time."

Addy commented skeptically, "OK… but don't wait too long." Just as I was nodding in agreement, I glanced out the window. Excitedly, I turned to Addy and said, "Look! I think the family moving in across the street is here!" We hurried outside to watch what was going on.

Coming around the corner was an awesome antique cream-colored sports car and a moving van, with a silver SUV behind them. All the vehicles pulled into the driveway across the street. Anxiously, we waited, wide-eyed and breathless, for the people to get out. Could there possibly be another girl our age in the family? I thought to myself, *Probably not.*

After the sports car came to a halt in the driveway, a tall man emerged from the driver's seat. From the other side, a teenage boy about fifteen or sixteen years old got out. Addy and I looked at each other, and we both grimaced in disgust.

Addy said, with a sour expression, "He's too old for me to want to be friends with, and he's not even cute."

I giggled. And then one door of the silver SUV swung open, and a girl got out. She seemed slightly older than us, but it was difficult to tell. I glanced at Addy questioningly. She immediately understood, shrugged her shoulders, and replied, "She could be the same age or maybe a year older. Don't worry, we'll find out soon enough."

Looking back at the activity across the street and hearing the shouting that was going on, I said to Addy, "Everyone is so busy unloading. We shouldn't annoy them—yet."

Addy laughed in agreement, and we just sat back and watched, hoping that we both might have found another new friend.

After talking for quite a while and watching the progress across the street, I inquired, "Do you think it's all right to go over there now and introduce ourselves?"

Addy replied cheerfully, "Sure, let's go!"

We walked quickly across the street together and knocked on the front door. The tall man—who we assumed was the father—opened the door and asked irritably, "What do you want? We're very busy today, as you can see!"

I was really nervous, but Addy, with her cheerful disposition, blurted out, "Hi, I'm Addy and this is Leira. We noticed that you have a daughter about our age. We just thought we could introduce ourselves and welcome her to the neighborhood. We promise not to take up too much time. I just moved in earlier this week. I know how crazy everything is the first few days."

After considering us for a moment, her father yelled, "Skye!"

Skye appeared at the screen door and gazed out at us. With a shy smile, she stepped out onto the porch.

I said, "Hi, I'm Leira, and I live across the street, and this is my new friend, Addy, who just moved in next door to me. We're both eleven and starting sixth grade on Monday at the same school. Do you know what school you'll be going to?"

Skye replied, "I'm going to be twelve in November. I'll be starting sixth grade on Monday at J. P. Something School."

Enthusiastically, I replied, "That's fantastic! We're all going to the same school. But we might not have the same classroom because there are three sixth grade classes. We won't find out until we get there. I love your name—it's so beautiful."

Skye replied, "Well, actually my real name is Skylar, but everyone just calls me Skye with an e at the end. Your names are cool too. I bet no one at school will have names like ours."

I said, "As far as I know, no one does."

The three of us talked awhile longer, but it became apparent that Skye definitely had to return to unpacking. Addy was expected home soon. We all agreed to try and meet on Sunday afternoon for another visit.

As Addy and I started walking away, I turned back to Skye and said, "Just wait until tomorrow when I have time to tell both of you all about the creepy things I know about Grimly Manor!"

Addy whipped her head toward me in astonishment, and Skye quickly asked, "Grimly Manor? What's that?"

Noticing Addy's eyes fixed on me, I gave a mischievous grin, then plunged on through by saying, "You'll both have to wait until tomorrow, when there's enough time for me to tell you about the weird things that happen there and about the manor's owner, who no one has ever seen, except with a mask!"

I quickened my pace back across the street. Addy asked a bit breathlessly, "Why did you say that about Grimly Manor? I wanted you to talk about it earlier, but you said, it wasn't the right time—or something like that." Addy, who was expectantly waiting for an answer, stopped at the hedges between our yards.

I looked at her, feeling a little ashamed and slightly confused, and I answered honestly, "I can't explain it, but after meeting you, and just now as we met Skye, I wasn't so afraid to talk about it. I'm sorry, Addy. Grimly Manor has been a frightening mystery to me for so long, but now that there are three of us, I somehow feel I can finally face my fears—with my two new friends. Does that sound stupid?"

Addy smiled and replied, "No! But now I can't wait until tomorrow to hear more about it! I'll call you after lunch!"

With her mother calling for her, she gave me a quick hug and ran off to her new house.

As I lay awake in bed that night, cuddled up with my favorite stuffed bear, I felt so happy to have found not only one friend, but two! Maybe now I could have a real adventure with them. Little did I know what real "adventure" was in our path. Suddenly, it occurred to me that I hadn't asked Skye which bedroom was hers. I hoped it was the turreted bedroom. It would be so awesome to have a sleepover up there sometime.

Chapter 3
Super Sunday

AFTER CHURCH THAT Sunday, I hurried through my ham-and-cheese sandwich with chips and a pickle. It was definitely not my favorite lunch, although I do love chips (and pickles on occasion). After I finished, I anxiously looked out the window to see if Skye or Addy were home. Skye's parents' car was there, so I asked my mom, "Can I go and see if Skye is home now?"

My mom promptly replied, "All right, but remember that they're just moving in, so don't make a nuisance of yourself."

I responded, "Don't worry, I won't bug them!" So I skipped across the street and knocked on Skye's door. Skye's brother eventually opened it. With a sneer, he harshly asked, "What do you want?"

I replied apprehensively, "Skye and I had planned to spend a few hours together today. Is she home?"

Her brother shouted, "Mom!" Within a moment or two, Skye's mother arrived at the front door. She had wavy golden-red hair and had a gracious smile. With a sparkle in her eyes, she asked in a melodious Irish accent, "Hi there. I'm Mrs. Finnegan. Can I help you?"

I beamed and replied, "Hello, Mrs. Finnegan. I'm Leira MacGregor from across the street. I met Skye yesterday, and I was hoping that she'd be able to come over and visit with me for a couple of hours. Would that be all right?"

Her mom responded, "That's fine. She told us about you and Addy last night. She was extremely happy to meet two friendly girls her own age. But she'll need to be home by five o'clock for dinner."

I said, "That's no problem. Thanks, Mrs. Finnegan."

Skye was standing hesitantly in the background, waiting for her mom's response. When she heard it, she passed her mom on the way out the door saying, "Thanks, Mom! I'll be home by five!" We both walked happily over to my house.

Skye asked, "Is Addy coming over too?"

I replied, "I don't think she's home from church yet, but she told me yesterday that she thought she'd be able to come over after lunch. Let's stay outside on my porch so we can see when she gets home."

While we were sitting on the front steps, Skye asked, "What about this Grimly Manor that you mentioned yesterday? You made it sound kind of creepy."

I told her I thought we should wait until Addy was with us, so we could talk about it together. Then I asked Skye, "Which room in the house is yours? Do you have the cool room with the turret?"

She gave a little grimace and said, "No. My brother Liam and I started arguing about it so much that my mom decided neither of us could have it. She said that she was going to make it into a special guest bedroom."

I asked, "Well, which one is your room then?"

Skye replied, pointing, "It's the one on the left, on the second floor. Actually, it's really awesome, other than the fact that Liam shares the bathroom that connects our rooms. At least there are locks on the doors. In our last house, we had to share a room with bunk beds. It was gruesome, so I guess I shouldn't complain."

I said, "I've got the same room as yours, but your house was added on to a lot by the last owners, so I think it's probably much different than mine inside." I added, "I don't have any brothers or sisters, so I don't know much about sharing things. My parents bought our house the year I was born, so I guess in some ways I've been lucky to have my own room and my own bathroom."

Just then, I let my hair down from the bun I usually kept it in during the summer months. After releasing it and running my fingers through the honey brown strands, Skye stared in amazement and stated, "Whoa! You've got the longest hair I've ever seen!"

I blushed and replied, "Thanks. Most of the time, I put it up in different hairdos. My mom loves the things I come up with."

Changing the subject, I asked, "Do you like Beanie Babies? Addy and I both have quite a collection."

Skye replied, "I think they are really adorable, but I don't have very many. My favorite one 'disappeared,' if you know what I mean."

With a perplexed look I said, "No, I'm not sure I do know what you mean."

She glanced away for a significant moment and then, with a bit of anger in her voice, she said, "My older brother Liam is a terror. I can't prove it to my parents, but I just know he stole it and threw it away somewhere. He's always picking on me. That's one of the reasons I don't have many things. He always does something to them."

I looked at her in astonishment and declared, "That's horrible! Don't your parents ground him or something like that?"

Skye replied in resignation, "Well, yes, but only if they catch him. Unfortunately, there is only one thing he's really good at, in addition to picking on me, and that is not getting caught."

At that instant, we heard a car coming around the corner. The Davies' car pulled into their driveway, and everyone got out. I was relieved that Addy was home because I was hoping that the two of us could cheer up Skye. She appeared a bit sad after her confession. We waited about fifteen minutes and then walked over to the Davies' house.

We knocked on the door, and as it opened, a cute little dog greeted us by barking constantly while jumping up at us. Mrs. Davies, who was slim with short dark brown hair and beautiful deep brown eyes, gently pushed the dog away and said, "Hi, Leira."

I replied, "Hi, Mrs. Davies. This is Skye Finnegan, who just moved in yesterday, and we wondered if Addy could come over for a while?"

Mrs. Davies said, "I guess that's all right, but she has to be back in three hours to finish getting everything ready for school tomorrow." When Addy came hurrying out the door, she had that enormous smile on her face.

As Addy, Skye, and I walked back to my house, we decided to sit and talk on the front porch so we could have some privacy, while still enjoying the breezy, warm day. Before I was even able to sit down, Addy burst out, "Well? What is this stuff about Grimly Manor? Tell us everything you know!" Skye looked on in eager anticipation.

Chapter 2
Grimly Manor

SKYE AND ADDY sat on the porch with their attention riveted on me as I began to explain. "Here's what I know about Grimly Manor and some rumors I've heard."

Glancing up the street, I continued, "Do both of you see that old, creepy three-story house with the turrets at the end of the street?"

They both looked to where I was pointing and said hesitantly, "Yes."

"Well," I said a bit apprehensive, "that's Grimly Manor, and behind it is an ancient cemetery. If you look carefully, you can see some of the gravestones off to the left of the manor."

Both Addy and Skye turned their heads in the direction of Grimly Manor, searching for the gravestones. Addy was the first to break the silence by exclaiming, "Oh yeah! I see a whole bunch of them. That's really spooky, and my house is closer than yours!"

Skye squinted harder and then added, "I can sort of see them, but I think I need new glasses."

I waited a bit, and when they turned back to me, with apprehension filling their eyes, I continued. "Anyway, over the last two hundred years, the manor has only been owned by Grimlys. One of the things that's really eerie is that all the owners not only took care of the cemetery but were morticians as well!"

Perplexed, Skye asked, "Morticians? What are those?"

I replied, "You know, the people that fix up dead bodies and get them ready to be buried—it was all done at that manor. I think they also used to call them undertakers."

Skye and Addy looked horrified. Addy grimaced and asked, "Is that why the name of our street is Cemetery Street?"

"Yes," I replied. "You see, a long time ago, before our homes were built, there were several beautiful mansions in this neighborhood. Eventually most of them became deserted and fell apart, except Grimly Manor. After quite a while, a company came to tear down the ruins and build new homes—meaning ours. I think it was about twelve or thirteen years ago. Anyway, the builder was able to buy all the properties except the land with the cemetery and Grimly Manor. According to town laws about the manor, it was attached to the cemetery and as long as a Grimly descendant was alive, the manor could not be sold."

We suddenly heard the pounding of feet quickly approaching from the left. With our nerves on edge, all three of us whipped around with a jerk of fear.

We breathed a sigh of relief because it was only Josie, Addy's little sister.

She bounced up and down and asked excitedly, "Can I stay with you, Addy? I'm really bored, and you look like you're talking about something really cool."

Addy said with exasperation, "Not right now, Josie. I'm just getting to know my new friends. Maybe we can play later."

"Aaw," said Josie, "I never get to play with you when you're with your friends." Josie stomped away, her head hung low, and I felt a bit sorry for her.

Addy said, "Don't worry about her. She'll find new friends and won't be bothering us much longer—I hope."

I replied to Addy with a raised eyebrow, "I'm not sure about that because I don't know of any kids around here that are her age. Anyway, let me get on with the story. So all the mansions were bulldozed to the ground, and they built our awesome homes. Honestly, though, if you think about it, the original manors must have been incredible when they were new."

Skye inquired, "Were all the places as big as Grimly Manor?"

I said, with some hesitancy, "I'm not exactly sure. My parents moved here right before I was born, so I never saw any of them. But we could probably go to the town hall or library and find some pictures. Would you guys like to do that sometime?"

Skye nodded her head. Then Addy responded with a bright idea. "I think it would make a terrific history project, and I bet we would all get an A on it because we're so interested in it!"

I replied, "That's a good idea. But besides that, here's what I know personally about Grimly Manor. There's an old man living there—a Grimly, of course. Some people call him a recluse because no one ever sees him, with the exception of Halloween. But he's always wearing a mask when he opens the door, so no one really knows what he looks like!"

I continued, "His parents died when he was young, and he went off to live somewhere else until he grew up. Then he returned to take care of the manor. And get this—he doesn't have any electricity, gas, water, cable, or even a telephone! Our mail carrier, Bertha, once told me that he hardly ever gets any mail except for that stuff addressed to 'Resident' that everyone gets. Occasionally, at night you'll see flickering from candles in the windows and his shadow crossing a room. But how do you think he gets his food and from where? How could he possibly keep food without a refrigerator? Over the years, young kids and even teenagers have dared each other to go up and knock on the door. Most of them won't do it, but whenever someone gets brave enough, the only thing they hear is the snarling of a vicious animal!"

Addy gasped, "Oh my gosh! I could never do that!"

I continued, "Well, wait until you hear what happens on holidays. It gets even weirder. Before every holiday, you'll see the manor during the day, and it looks exactly the same as always. But then, one morning you'll wake up to find it completely decorated—to the max! Whether it's Christmas, Halloween, Easter, or whatever, all these things appear like magic. It's always so brilliant! I can't wait until you can see it for yourselves. The confusing part is that you never know if it will happen a month before the holiday or the night before, but it always happens, and no one so far has been able to see how it's done and who does it!"

Suddenly, Josie came racing across the yard and stopped in front of us. With her hands on her hips, she yelled at Addy, "You have to come home now! Mom and Dad say that you have to come help me get ready for school!"

Addy, looking quite irritated, angrily exclaimed, "Mom said I could stay for three hours. It hasn't even been two. What's the deal?"

Josie, smirking happily, replied, "I don't know. That's just what Mom told me. You have to come home now." With a look of triumph on her face, she spun around and headed back to their house.

Addy looked at me after Josie started toward home and said, "Well, I don't know why I have to go, but I do. If she's lying to me, I'll come right back. I don't want to leave. This story is so creepy! I hope I don't have trouble falling asleep tonight."

Skye teased her by saying, "I'd be more worried about nightmares if I were you!"

Addy replied sarcastically, "Thanks a lot, Skye! Now I'll never get to sleep!"

Then looking at me, Addy said, "Tomorrow is the first day of school, and my mom said I can walk with you and Skye. Do you think that will be all right with your parents?"

I replied, "My mom has already said OK. What about you, Skye?"

Skye replied, "I'll call and let you know. I'm sure it will be fine."

Addy asked, "So I'll meet you and possibly Skye at the corner around seven thirty in the morning? Then, on the way to school, you can tell us some more about the manor, Leira."

I responded, "Yeah, that sounds good to me. But don't worry if it's raining or something because my mom can drive us before she goes to work."

Skye said, "Well, I hope it doesn't rain because I really want to walk to school." We exchanged phone numbers, and Addy went home. Skye stayed until five o'clock, and we chatted about the neighborhood and what our school was like. I wouldn't answer any more questions about Grimly Manor as I felt it wasn't fair to Addy. After Skye left, I felt as though I had just experienced the best day of my life!

I had no idea that during the next week someone would actually go to Grimly Manor and knock on the door!

Chapter 5
The First Day of School!

I WOKE UP early Monday morning, and I was so excited that my alarm didn't even have to wake me up. I amazed my mom by getting my own breakfast (my favorite cereal and Nana's bread, a special kind of bread my Nana bakes for me). I even got my lunch ready. Actually, it was simple because I was going to get a hot lunch at school. They were having chicken nuggets and potato puffs, which were some of the few things I liked. So all I needed was a healthy snack and a drink. I was ready fifteen minutes early.

When my mom came back after her daily morning run and glanced at my backpack, she noticed it was ready to go and that I was putting on my new furry fall jacket. As she picked up her running towel and began swabbing the sweat from her face, she breathlessly asked, "What has got you in such a hurry this morning?"

I reminded her that I was meeting Addy and Skye to walk to school. I asked, "Don't you remember me asking you yesterday if I could?"

She gave me an exhausted smile and replied, "I'm happy you've got friends to walk to school with. But don't forget, I'll drive you if the weather is bad." Then she asked, "Is Addy's little sister walking to school with you?"

I replied, "No—not yet. Mrs. Davies wants her to wait until she's older."

Cheerfully, Mom replied, "Have a great first day of school. Don't forget to bring home all my 'homework.' I always get so many papers to fill out. Do you have your lunch money?"

I responded slyly, "Of course I do, but you can always give me more!"

Mom gave me that look of "Yeah, right." Afterward, she reached over and gave me an enormous hug and then headed off for a shower.

I quickly left the house and hurried to the corner. Addy and Skye were already waiting. I was delighted! We greeted each other like we had been close friends for years. It was a fantastic way to begin a new year at school.

On our walk to school, which was a little less than a mile away, Skye said without any apprehension, "Maybe we should go knock on the door of Grimly Manor today. What do you think?"

Addy and I looked at Skye in astonishment!

Addy came to an abrupt halt and stammered, "What? Are you serious? Why on earth would we do that? It's only the first day of school. I don't want to spend the day worrying about that. Besides, even if we did, what would happen if he answers? What the heck would we say? Never mind what would happen if he lets his hideous animal loose on us. Definitely not!" Then after seeing the look on Skye's face, she added, "Well, at least not today, anyway."

Skye answered reasonably, "Well, according to Leira, nothing really terrible has happened. There's just been a growling dog or something. I think we should check it out. Besides, Halloween is next month, and we'll certainly knock on his door then. So why don't we try it now?"

I was completely shocked! I burst out, "Skye, aren't you the least bit afraid?"

She immediately replied, "No, not as long as both of you are with me."

I shuffled my feet on the cracked pavement and finally said, "I think Addy's right, but why don't we decide on the way home?" Addy appeared more at ease after that.

Skye replied, "All right, I guess we have enough to think about right now." Then she asked me, "Is there anything else you can tell us about Mr. Grimly or the manor?"

I replied, "There are several rumors, but I don't know if I would actually believe most of them. Some of the older kids might just be trying to scare the younger ones with stories they make up."

"Like what?" Addy asked.

My reoccurring nightmare flashed through my thoughts as I replied, "Well, one of the most outrageous tales is that during the night, he goes out into the cemetery, digs up corpses, and carries them back into the manor." I saw Addy's eyes widen in horror, so I quickly added, "I really doubt that it's true because everyone claims he never leaves the manor."

Skye asked, "What do they say he does with the bodies?"

Addy let out a groan of fright, and for a moment, I thought she was going to faint. I quickly answered, "Well, I'm sure the older boys could come up with a lot of gruesome answers to that, but like I said before, I don't believe any of it is true. The kid who started that rumor knocked on the door earlier this year and ended up running away, terrified. Some kids saw it happen, so I think that he made up the story to scare everyone. That way, they'd be too afraid to prove him wrong and figure out that he's really just a coward. I don't think anyone's knocked on the door since then."

Addy responded tremulously, "What if the rumor is true? You said he never comes out of the manor. But you also can't explain how the place gets decorated."

I gazed at Addy calmly and replied, "Once you know more about this kid that made up the rumor, you won't believe him either. He's a troublemaker and a bully. I guess he has problems, but no one will stand up to him because he might retaliate."

Skye looked confused and asked, "What does *retaliate* mean?"

I replied, "You know, it's like getting back at someone, hurting them or doing something to their house. No one wants to get this kid mad at them because he's really big and nasty."

Skye chuckled and said, "Well, we're going to find out exactly what's going on at Grimly Manor, and when we do, we'll show everyone that he's a liar and a scaredy-cat! Besides, my brother Liam is a big guy too, and I'm positive he'd keep that kid from hurting us in any way. So what did you say this kid's name is?"

"I didn't say, but his name is Frankie," I replied cautiously.

Addy and I glanced at each other worriedly, and I wondered just what I was getting myself into. I was definitely interested to learn more about Mr. Grimly and his manor, but I absolutely didn't want Frankie angry with us. I looked at Skye and asked, "You said your brother is horrible to you, so why would he protect you?"

Skye smirked and said, "Well, actually, Liam tortures me at times, but—he doesn't want anyone else doing it. I think it's his weird idea of family pride or something. I'm not sure how else to explain it, but he wouldn't let Frankie do anything to us."

I said skeptically, "Well, that makes me feel a little better." Turning to Addy, I said, "I can't answer your question about how Mr. Grimly puts up the holiday decorations, Addy, but maybe together, the three of us will be able to find out."

We began heading down the school driveway. We were suddenly more nervous about school than anything else. After entering the front doors, Skye and Addy went to the office to find out which rooms they were in. I had to go straight to my class. Happily, Skye appeared after several minutes at my classroom door. We both had Mrs. Pollock for a teacher. She was very nice, tall, and pretty, with beautiful long blond hair. She had just gotten married during the summer.

Much to Addy's disappointment, she had a different teacher. Her name was Ms. Oldman, but she wasn't old. I had heard she was a fantastic teacher and could be a bit silly at times.

The first day of school was scary and fun at the same time. Mrs. Pollock arranged our seating charts alphabetically, and Skye ended up sitting next to me! Also, there were two boys that had been kind of nice to me over the last several years who were in our class. One of them sat in front of me.

We had music class that day, so Skye got to meet Mr. Balhooner, who was also the minister of music at my church. I had told Skye and Addy all about him, and after music class was over, she said, "You're right. He's really awesome! I'm going to ask my mom if I can go to church with you and join the choir. After what you've told me and now having had class today with him, I really want to join."

After the ending school bell rang, the three of us regrouped to walk home and discuss our day. Addy exclaimed, "Ms. Oldman is terrific—and really funny! She's also very young, if you hadn't noticed.

All I have for homework is to cover my books. She even complimented me on my handwriting."

Addy then continued less cheerfully, "Unfortunately, not everything went so well. There's this kid named Jeffrey in my class. He's horrible. And not only that, but Ms. Oldman paired him up with me! I always seem to get stuck with the rotten kids. Then, on top of that, there's this girl named Brenda in my class that never stops talking and fooling around. She even shot a hair tie at me today! It was lucky for her that Ms. Oldman didn't see her, but I wish she had!"

I replied sympathetically, "I know how you feel because Jeffrey was in my class last year. He's an annoying little idiot, and I've heard about how bad Brenda is. She was a new student last year, but she wasn't in my classroom. The best thing to do is just ignore them. Hopefully, they won't pick on you, especially after they find out the three of us are friends."

Addy stated, "I've always been an A student, and I hope they don't mess things up for me."

I said confidently, "Don't worry, you'll do fine."

Addy thanked me as we continued walking home.

Our first day of school was over, but the most petrifying part of the day was about to begin!

Chapter 6
A Knock on the Door

IT WAS A bright, sunny day and extremely warm for September. We were about halfway home when I said to Skye and Addy, "My pool is still open! Do you think you could go swimming after your homework is finished? It's solar-heated, so it's really warm."

Skye raised her eyebrows and grinned, stating, "I think my mother will say yes, but I don't know where my bathing suit is."

I replied enthusiastically, "That's all right! My mom and I have a bunch of suits. I'm sure we'll find something, even if it might need a couple of safety pins."

Addy giggled and said, "Well, I've finished my unpacking, so I know right where mine is."

Just then, we came around the curve in the road where Cemetery Street began. Nearing Grimly Manor, Skye asked, "Well, are we going to stop at Grimly Manor today? We're all in such a terrific mood that nothing could spoil it—right?"

Addy and I glanced at each other nervously. Trying not to sound intimidated, I suggested to Skye, "Why don't we stop another time? This might be the last day warm enough to go swimming."

Addy rapidly added, "Yeah, I agree with Leira. Let's just go swimming. We can stop at Grimly Manor some other day, when it's colder."

Skye squinted and asked, "You're both chickening out, aren't you? Besides, it'll only take a few minutes. Let's just get it over with. And just think," she added teasingly, "we might be dripping in sweat after our 'terrifying' experience, and the swimming pool will feel even better then." She looked at us expectantly for an answer.

Addy and I felt like cowards, but ultimately stated, "All right." I added, "Let's hurry up before I lose my nerve."

Then Addy inquired with trepidation, "What are we going to do if he answers the door? Do you have any suggestions?"

Skye and I looked at each other, and I hesitantly replied, "Well, he's never done that before—except on Halloween. But if he does, I could probably just say that I wanted to introduce both of you to him because you just moved into the neighborhood."

Addy, looking extremely surprised, asked, "You would say that?"

Gulping, I replied, "Well, if Skye is brave enough to knock on the door, then I think I'm prepared to say just about anything." Then I added in an anxious tone, "But be ready for the snarling whatever."

As we closed in on the manor, I could sense the anxiety we were all feeling. We kept on walking though, and as we turned up the driveway, the cemetery in the back felt like it was creeping toward us. With every step we took, the tingles went faster up and down my spine. My heart was pounding, and I could hear Addy's breathing becoming louder and quicker. The three of us hesitantly approached the front porch steps, which were covered with weeds and vines. Some of the wood was definitely starting to decay. I had never felt so petrified in my life. When we reached the old warped door, Skye took a deep breath and knocked slowly three times. With each bang of her fist hitting the door, Addy and I took a small step backward.

Suddenly, the air was split with a ferocious growling from behind the door! The three of us backed down to the bottom of the steps and stared at each other. With terror in my eyes, I shakily said, "OK, why don't we try this some other time? I would much rather be swimming."

Skye looked at us both, and even though the snarling was still going on, she said with determination, "I'm going to try one more time!"

Addy and I stayed firmly where we were and glanced at each other fearfully. I could see the sweat popping out on Addy's forehead and sensed the exact thing happening on me. As Skye approached the door, she noticed a sheet of paper partially shoved inside the rickety screen door. Hesitantly, she pulled it out and brought it to us.

Addy shrieked in horror, "What the heck are you doing? Put that back immediately—it's private!"

Skye smirked at us both and replied, "It's a grocery list. Look."

Somewhat relieved, I asked, "What—a grocery list?" Briefly gathering my thoughts, I said, "Well, that explains part of how he gets his food." Then immediately I told Skye, "Hurry, put it back before we are discovered. We'd better leave here before something bad happens."

Skye challenged teasingly, "Are you absolutely sure? I'll knock one more time if you want me to."

Both Addy and I quickly responded, "NO!"

The three of us turned around and hurried away from Grimly Manor, feeling a little foolish. Breathlessly, I said to Skye, "Whoa! That was either really brave of you or really stupid. I'm not sure which, but I wish I were more like you."

Skye replied, "Just remember, I have an older brother that I've had to deal with all my life, and he can be seriously scary. I haven't had any choice but to learn to stand up to him. Look on the bright side, we don't have to live with Mr. Grimly."

Addy and I both laughed at that remark and felt much better about ourselves. As we finished walking home, I said, "Obviously someone is picking up the list and delivering the food, but I wonder who does it, and when? Maybe if we could keep watch, somehow we'd be able to find out. Let's talk about it later. I hope you can both go swimming with me."

Both Skye's and Addy's moms said it was all right for them to come over after they completed their homework. I sprinted home and pulled out all the paperwork my mom had to go through. After that, I quickly searched through her dresser drawer and found a swimsuit I thought would fit Skye. I grabbed some towels, went out back to the pool, and rolled back the solar cover. Warming myself on the sunny deck, I went over the day's events in my head. So much had happened!

Just then, Skye and Addy arrived. I handed Skye the swimsuit, and she went into the house to change. I skimmed the pool a little while Addy climbed the ladder. Shortly after, Skye appeared, and the two of us climbed up onto the deck.

Addy laughed and said, "This is really awesome. I used to live in Wisconsin, and there was no way you could go swimming, even in the summer! Well, you could, but the water was freezing. No one in our neighborhood had a heated pool."

I asked her, "How come your parents chose to move to Connecticut?"

As she lowered herself into the water, Addy promptly replied, "Well, my dad got a huge promotion, but to get it, we had to move to Connecticut. We didn't mind moving, because with his promotion, we were able to buy our new house. It's much nicer than the one we lived in before."

I exclaimed, "That's terrific! Especially for me. How about you, Skye? Why did you move here?"

Skye grinned and said, "Well, we used to live in a crummy little house in Virginia. But you're not going to believe this: my dad won the lottery, for two million dollars! We were going to stay in Virginia and move to a nicer neighborhood, but everyone knew we had won the money, and people started bugging us. So my mom convinced my dad to move here because she has family nearby."

Addy interrupted, "What do you mean by 'bugging us'? What happened?"

Skye answered thoughtfully, "Well, first, the phone never seemed to stop ringing. All kinds of other people kept calling, trying to get us to buy stuff or give money. Even though we got our phone number changed, within a week, the calls started coming again. Also, there were a lot of creepy people coming to the door. Even some of our relatives that we hadn't heard from in years began calling and writing." I asked, "Wasn't anyone nice?"

Skye replied, "Yeah. We had some really good friends in our neighborhood that weren't happy we were leaving and a few relatives that we usually got together with. I think they'll come and visit sometime. But anyway, I think the whole thing was a really bad experience—except for the money, of course. Anyway, some real estate guy found us this place, and even though we didn't need such a large house, my mom now has her dream home. I'm so happy we moved here because now I have both of you for friends."

I replied, "That's an incredible story. I've never met anyone who's won the lottery before! It must be fate—or something—that brought the three of us together." Changing the subject, I said, "I still can't believe that you actually went back to Mr. Grimly's door and pulled out that list! You have a lot more nerve than I do."

Skye said, "Not really. To tell you the truth, I was scared to death. But I didn't want to back down, especially in front of you guys."

With the three of us laughing, Skye and I both jumped into the pool with a huge splash. We had a fantastic time! But that night, lying awake, I wondered just how much more of an adventure this would turn into. Today had been really scary for me, but it had also been kind of exciting. I wondered what would happen next.

Chapter 7
Buttering Up Our Parents!

TUESDAY MORNING WHILE walking to school, I asked Skye and Addy, "Do you have any ideas about how we could keep watch on the manor? Someone should be delivering his groceries during the week. Don't you think so?"

Addy immediately replied, "Yes, and we know that he doesn't get any deliveries during the day, or at least no one's seen it, if he did. What if we take turns staying up during the night to watch his house?"

I thought about it for few moments and responded, "Well, I guess we could try that. But we'll have to figure out who's going to watch at what time. I mean, we can't possibly stay awake too long or we won't be able to get up in the morning."

I continued, "The street curves a little, so I've got a really good view of the manor from my front bedroom window."

Skye stated, "My room is exactly the opposite of yours, but if I look out the side window, I can see the manor perfectly!"

Addy said dismally, "I have a big problem. I really can't see Grimly Manor from my bedroom."

I responded disappointedly, "There's no way Skye and I can watch the manor by ourselves."

Skye considered that and replied, "You're right about that." Then she added sarcastically, "Does anyone have another smart idea?"

Addy suggested, "Let's think about it for a couple of days. I'm sure that between the three of us, we'll come up with a different plan." Skye and I agreed.

During the rest of the week, we batted around ideas about how we could keep watch on Grimly Manor. After a few days, I came up with a suggestion I thought might work. I asked Skye and Addy, "What if we have a sleepover at my house on the weekend and stay up until morning keeping watch?"

Skye and Addy thought this was a good idea, but then Skye commented, "We can't be sure that anything will happen that night."

I responded, "I know, but maybe over the next month or so we could do a few more sleepovers, at each other's houses on different nights. That way, we might find out more information—or at the very least, figure out which nights nothing happens."

Addy commented, "This all sounds like an excellent plan, but first we have to soften up our parents or it will never happen."

Skye and I agreed, so on Thursday after school, we went straight to my house and immediately began planning our strategies.

On Friday after school, I knew my mom wouldn't be home for at least an hour and a half, so during that time, I cleaned my room, washed the dishes, and ironed everything in the laundry basket. It was really hard work, but I was pretty sure my mom wouldn't say no after all that. I knew she hated ironing, especially my dad's shirts. I was thinking about what else I might do to soften her up, when I heard her car pull into the driveway. I thought, *Oh well, here it goes. I hope I didn't do all this work for nothing.*

Addy, in contrast, raced home, tidied her room, and cleaned her hamsters' cage. After playing games with Josie on the Internet for a while, she asked her mom if she could help make dinner.

Her mother was speechless! She replied, "Addy, you've really brightened my day. Thank you so much, for playing with Josie, and yes, I'd love someone help making dinner. Could you make the salad to go with the shepherd's pie? Just slice up that head of lettuce and add some cherry tomatoes and cucumbers. Can you manage that?"

Addy replied with a cheerful smile, "Sure!" They always had dinner early so she still had plenty of time to pop the big question later.

Meanwhile, Skye got home and discovered that her brother Liam was the only one there. She gave him a scornful look, hurried past him, and went straight to her room. She cleaned it up, spick-and-span! Next, she sneakily packed her overnight bag, predicting that everything would go according to plan. Finally, she did the best thing of all for her mother. Skye scooped up all the dirty laundry around the entire house, brought it downstairs, and sorted it. She even started the first washer load of clothes. Her mother had only shown her how to do it a couple of times, but she thought she did it just right. When Skye's mom arrived home at five o'clock, Skye casually explained what she had finished doing.

Her mother looked at her in amazement and suspiciously asked, "Skye, what's going on? Don't get me wrong, I'm very proud of you, but do you have some special reason for doing all this?"

So... everything was set to spring the big question on each of our mothers.

When Skye finally answered her mother's question, she said, "Well, the reason is that Leira asked if I could sleep over her house tonight, and I really want to! Is it all right with you?"

Her mother responded, "Absolutely, I'm so happy you and Leira have become good friends! Pack up your sleepover things and you can leave as soon as she calls. Oh, one other thing—I'd like to speak to Mr. or Mrs. MacGregor when Leira phones." Then her mom gave her a big hug and said, "You didn't need to do all that, but I'm very grateful you did."

Skye thanked her mom and went to supposedly gather her stuff for the sleepover.

Addy didn't have any difficulty either when she asked her mom. Mrs. Davies replied knowingly, "I wondered why you were being extra helpful. Yes, you can sleep over."

Addy thanked and hugged her mom then headed off to her bedroom to pack her sleepover bag and called to let me know she could come. She asked, "Is there anything special I should bring?"

I replied, "I can't think of anything right now, even though I've probably forgotten something. By the way, Skye called and said she'd be coming over as soon as I call and tell her that everything's all set. So don't come over until you hear from me. It'll be really embarrassing if my mom says no. I'm going to go ask now. Wish me luck."

Then came the big moment for me! When my mother came through the door, I told her all the wonderful things I'd done for her.

She immediately asked, "OK, what is it that you want? You would never do all this without a catch."

Looking innocently at my mom, I pleaded in my sweetest voice, "Can Skye and Addy please sleep over tonight? We really want to sleep in the living room with the new wide-screen plasma TV. We promise to keep the volume down. I've never had a sleepover, and we won't disturb you or Dad. They've already had supper so they won't need to eat—well, except for some snacks and drinks. Please… can they sleep over?"

My mom studied me for a moment, smiled, and replied, "Well, this tactic of yours won't work every time, but yes, they can sleep over. And in the morning, we'll take everyone out for breakfast."

At last, everything was set! I called Skye first, and my mom and Mrs. Finnegan chatted for a while, before she told Skye she could leave for the sleepover. Afterward, I phoned Addy. They both arrived around seven o'clock. We began arranging the living room for the sleepover (ha-ha). Skye and Addy took the sleeper sofa, and I had a cot with a comfy sleeping bag. With the large grandfather clock in the corner, we could easily keep track of the time. It chimed loudly on the hour and once on the half hour, which might help keep us awake. We were ready for the night's adventure to begin!

Chapter 8
A Light in the Cemetery

FOR THE FIRST two hours of the night, we decided to watch a scary movie. My parents knew that the three of us liked that kind of movie, so I was pretty sure they wouldn't suspect anything. I asked Skye and Addy, "Why don't you each pick out two movies and then I'll choose which one to watch first?" Skye and Addy headed off to the media cabinet in the family room and came back a few minutes later with their selection of movies. I chose the one I thought would certainly set the mood for what we were about to do. It was about a haunted mansion. I told them, "This is a fantastic movie, and one of my favorite actors stars in it."

Addy asked curiously, "Oh really? And who might that be?"

Slightly embarrassed, I replied, "Well, I'm not saying, but you'll probably figure it out once we start watching it." Before starting the DVD, we made my favorite buttery popcorn. As Skye brought the bowl into the living room, Addy and I grabbed three sodas with lots of caffeine in them from the fridge. We were hoping that would help keep us awake during the night.

My mom popped in on us at eight o'clock and asked if she could get us anything.

Politely, I replied, "No, we're all set, but thanks for asking."

At nine o'clock, we started another movie that wasn't as scary as the first one was. Mom showed up again and said to me, "Leira, Dad and I are going to bed to read for a while. Is there anything you girls need before we go?"

I responded brightly, "Nope! We're all fine right now, Mom. We're going to stay up for a while and finish watching this movie. Is it all right to put on another one if we aren't sleepy?"

Mom replied, "Well, as long as it's not too scary or too long. Remember, we're going out to brunch tomorrow morning around ten thirty, so I don't want to hear any complaints. One more thing—keep the volume down, and if either Addy or Skye want to go to sleep, then use the earphones. Is that understood?"

I replied, "OK, we'll see you in the morning."

She nodded and went upstairs.

After she left I said, "All right, it's time to put our plan into motion.

I stayed up late last night, so I'll try and get a couple of hours of sleep first, while both of you keep a lookout." Then I picked up three pieces of paper, handed one to both Skye and Addy, and said, "Here's the schedule I made up of who will be watching and at what times. I thought this would be easier than just trying to remember, because the longer we're awake, the fuzzier things might get. This chart should really help. Are there any questions?" As Skye and Addy carefully looked over their charts, I added, "There will either be one or two of us awake at all times."

Apparently, the schedule made sense because Addy nodded, and Skye smiled and said, "Got it! You did a great job on this, Leira! We could probably use this on a school project or something."

Raising my eyebrows, I replied, "Thanks, Skye, I'll keep that in mind as I try and fall asleep."

Although they were supposedly watching the movie, Skye and Addy were actually gazing out the window at Grimly Manor.

Addy stayed up with Skye for the next hour. While they were 'watching' the movie, Addy asked Skye, "Did you have any special friends in Virginia that you had to leave behind when you moved here?"

Skye replied, "Well, not exactly. That's why I'm so happy we've moved here! What about you? Did you have special friends you had to leave?"

Addy yawned and replied, "Not especially. Right now, I'm so tired that I'd rather talk about it tomorrow. It's ten o'clock, so I guess that means I can crawl into bed for two hours. Make sure you tell Leira to wake me up at midnight and *don't* fall asleep!"

Nothing happened at Grimly Manor between nine and eleven o'clock. Skye woke me up promptly at eleven and said, "It's your turn." Gazing at my droopy eyelids, she asked, "Are you sure you're awake enough?"

Stifling a yawn, I responded, "Yep, I think so. I'll get a soda and wake up Addy in another hour and then we can help keep each other awake." I rolled off my cot, and instead of going to the kitchen for a drink as I had intended, I stumbled to the window. Skye, thinking ahead, had a soda to hand me. Feeling a bit embarrassed, I thanked her then grabbed the bag of chips and a big container of sour cream to dip them in and plunked down in my favorite comfy chair. After taking a couple of salty, creamy bites, I began gazing out the window toward Grimly Manor. I was glad my dog, Lucky, wasn't sleeping downstairs. Mom and Dad had made sure she was upstairs in their bedroom with them.

After quite a while of squinting out the window at the manor, I saw the dim light of a flickering candle downstairs. Suddenly wide awake, I thought, *I can't believe this is happening!* It felt like I was dreaming, but the taste of the potato chips and icy cold soda told me I wasn't. This was so exciting! I wondered what Mr. Grimly was doing. I couldn't imagine what reason he had for being up so late. It was nearly midnight.

Slapping my hand over my mouth, I thought to myself, *What if he's actually watching me?* It was an extremely creepy thought that he might be doing just that. I suddenly felt slightly guilty about what we were doing. That idea instantly vanished as the clock struck midnight and started to chime twelve times.

Hurriedly, I walked over to Addy and tried to wake her up. I reached over again and briskly nudged her. When her eyes finally fluttered open, I whispered, "Addy, it's your turn to help keep me keep watch."

Rubbing her eyes, she reached for her drink and glanced toward the window. She asked wearily, "Have you seen anything happening yet?"

I replied, "No… well, yes. Since Skye went to sleep, I've seen candlelight flickering in several rooms on the first floor. It's been really spooky though, because I keep thinking he might be watching us back.

But honestly, nothing weird has happened. It's just that it's really creepy watching the manor alone, even though you guys are right here. I know he's there because of the candle lights moving from room to room. I'm beginning to wish we hadn't watched that scary movie after all."

Addy replied with a grimace, "Well, it's too late to think of that now. We'll know better next time."

Startled, I asked, "Next time?"

I had one more hour to stay awake, and as the time passed, my eyelids got heavier and heavier. It was forty-five minutes past twelve o'clock, with only a few minutes left before my watch was over, when Addy shoved me and said urgently, "Look!"

I blinked my eyes several times and was astounded to see a small light moving in the cemetery! I told Addy, "Quick! Hurry and wake up Skye!"

Addy raced over to Skye and shook her awake, but she kept her fingers to her lips reminding her to be quiet. Skye raced to the window where all three of us stared in amazement, trying to see exactly what was happening.

Addy said, "The light is swinging a bit, and it's moving toward the center of the cemetery."

"Darn," I said, "if only I could use my dad's binoculars, we'd be able to see everything! But not only will he not let me use them unless he's there, I don't even know where they are."

Skye suggested, "We could sneak outside and move closer!"

Both Addy and I gasped at once and whispered a bit loudly, "NO WAY!"

I stated, "First of all, my parents would kill me if they found out, and second, even if they didn't, I'd probably scare myself to death!"

Skye responded with a shrug, "Well, it was just a suggestion."

I confronted her in exasperation and demanded, "Where on earth do you get your courage from?"

Skye grinned and calmly replied, "I have both of you to protect me, don't I?"

Addy and I looked at each other and laughed softly. I put my finger up to my lips thoughtfully, then with a questioning look, I said,

"Hmm, let's see. Out of the three of us, you're the oldest, the biggest, and I would say, the strongest. Sooo it's kind of bizarre that the only reason you're so brave is that Addy and I are here to protect you. Who's going to protect us?"

Skye grinned again and stated simply, "Me, of course!" We laughed again.

We continued to watch the mysterious swinging light as it moved back toward the manor and then finally disappeared.

Skye said with a touch of enthusiasm, "I have a perfect idea! In a few weeks, it will be my birthday. So I'm going to ask my parents for a good pair of binoculars. Then, we can have another sleepover and see what's really going on!"

Both Addy and I nodded sleepily. Yawning, I asked Skye, "Are you going to have a birthday party or something?"

She replied, "I don't know yet. With the moving and everything, I don't think my parents have thought about it. Don't worry, though, I'll remind them."

We kept watching for more than another hour. By then, it was nearing two o'clock, and the three of us decided that we probably wouldn't see anything more. The candles in the manor had been extinguished shortly after the light in the cemetery disappeared. So the three of us climbed into our soft, cozy beds and pulled the covers way up, as we were all still a bit spooked. My last thought before I fell asleep was *I hope Mom and Dad don't get us up too early!*

Chapter 9
Weekend Woes and Monday Nightmares!

SATURDAY MORNING, MY mother tried unsuccessfully to get us up at nine o'clock. After several minutes, Addy slowly emerged from under her covers, and with a huge yawn said sleepily to my mom, "Good morning, Mrs. MacGregor." As my mother firmly nudged me awake once more, I responded in aggravation, "What? Leave me alone."

Irritably, Mom said, "You'll wake up right now and get both of your friends up! I told you yesterday that we're going out to breakfast this morning, and I definitely want the three of you ready in forty-five minutes. Is that perfectly understood?"

I immediately replied with a sour look, "OK!" Addy and I spent at least five minutes trying to wake up Skye. It wasn't until my dog, Lucky, came rushing into the living room and sprang up on her that she leapt out of bed.

Skye yelled in disgust, "What's that awful smell?"

I started laughing and said to Skye, "It's my dog, Lucky. Don't you remember that a skunk sprayed her a few weeks ago? Even though we've given her several tomato sauce baths, whenever it rains, she smells gross again. It must have rained sometime after we finally went to bed."

Addy had already moved away from Lucky and headed with her overnight bag to the bathroom to get dressed.

As Lucky jumped up at her once again, Skye shrieked, "Oh my gosh! That's so rancid."

To make matters worse, Lucky commenced mercilessly attacking Skye with licks and kisses. Skye screeched, "Get her off me!" The next thing I knew, Lucky was chasing Skye around the living room. I tried unsuccessfully to suppress the laughter bubbling up inside me, but giggling uncontrollably, I blurted out, "Don't worry, she just likes you!"

Skye promptly replied, "Well, I don't want her to like me, especially when she stinks so bad!" Skye grabbed her sleepover pack and flew to the bathroom with Lucky right behind her. Skye jiggled the bathroom doorknob urgently, but Addy had locked the door.

When Addy heard that someone was trying to enter, she stated indignantly, "I'm trying to get dressed."

Skye shouted to Addy, "I don't care! Just open the door!"

Addy yelled back, "Hang on—I'll be done in just a few minutes!"

I quickly approached Skye and urged, "Go upstairs. There's another bathroom there, or use the one in my bedroom." Skye hurried up the stairs as fast as she could. Fortunately, because Lucky was getting old, she couldn't follow quickly.

Soon after, Addy emerged from the bathroom and said, "Well, what's going on out here?"

After explaining, we both started to laugh hysterically. When Skye returned, she stated angrily, "You wouldn't have found it so funny if it had been you she leapt on! By the way, I was in the middle of a terrific dream too!"

"Oh really?" I asked intrigued. "And what was the dream about?"

Skye's face reddened, and she replied, embarrassed, "Well, if you're lucky, I'll tell you some other time. I'm not in the mood to tell you now, and we shouldn't keep your parents waiting any longer."

I laughed and teased, "If we're *Lucky?*"

Skye picked up the nearest pillow and threw it directly at me! Then she stated, "The next time Lucky comes in wet and stinky, I'll throw her at you instead of a pillow!"

Needless to say, we were extremely sleepy during breakfast. My parents eventually agreed to take us to my favorite diner, where I always got chocolate chip pancakes and bacon. When the waitress placed our dishes in front of us, even the heavenly aroma of sizzling bacon couldn't keep our eyelids from drooping.

Mom asked suspiciously, "How late did you stay up last night?"

Yawning, I replied, "I went to bed at nine o'clock."

Addy stated, "I went to sleep around ten."

My parents looked expectantly at Skye, and she stated smugly, "I stayed up and finished the movie—not like these two party poopers! I think I finally fell asleep about eleven."

My mother gazed intently at the three of us and asked, "Why are all of you so tired?"

I replied with a yawn, "Well, I think we might have woken up a few times during the night because we were so excited about the sleepover. So maybe we didn't get enough sleep. I think I'll take a short nap when we get home." Looking at Skye and Addy, I asked, "Doesn't that sound good to you?" They nodded in agreement.

Addy remarked, "Thank you, Mrs. MacGregor, for taking us out to breakfast." Yawning, she continued, "It's really very good."

The rest of the weekend passed by quickly. I was enthusiastic when Skye accompanied us to church on Sunday and asked to join the choir. Happily, the answer was yes. I couldn't wait until Wednesday night for our first choir practice of the year. Skye and I started planning a sneaky surprise for Mr. Balhooner!

Monday morning eventually arrived, and since the weather was nice, we walked to school. Skye and I had phys. ed. that day, and Addy had library and reading buddies. Skye and I had a terrific day, with the exception of math, which we both had a hard time with. The three of us were lucky to get an excellent teacher for PE, otherwise known as phys. ed. I've had her ever since I started kindergarten. We played volleyball that day. I wasn't very good at it, and Mrs. Quartz said I needed to be more aggressive. I definitely needed to work on that. But Skye was astonishing!

During lunch, Skye and I noticed that Addy appeared rather upset. Usually, the three of us had recess together, but because of PE, our class missed it.

We met outside after school, and as we started walking home, I softly asked Addy, "What happened today? You looked upset at lunch. Is there anything we can do?"

Addy tersely replied, "I don't want to talk about it right now."

Skye consolingly said, "Hey, we're best friends now. You can tell us anything. We'll do everything we can do to help, and we promise to keep whatever you say secret." Skye turned to me and asked, "Right, Leira?"

I encouraged Addy by saying, "Absolutely, your secrets are safe with us. We really want to help."

Addy took a deep breath and said, "All right, I'll tell you, but you both have to <u>swear</u> that you won't repeat a word to anyone." Skye and I gave her our solemn promises not to utter a peep.

"Well," Addy began tentatively, "you know that awful kid Jeffrey in my class?"

Skye and I nodded, and then Skye asked cautiously, "What did he do to you?"

Addy immediately replied, "He didn't really *do* anything to me. He told me how much he loved my beautiful black hair and then he asked me to go out with him!"

Skye and I gasped!

Addy continued, "I told him my mother wouldn't let me go out with anyone while I'm in sixth grade. Even though I was telling him the truth, the fact is, I would never go out with him. He's so gross and nasty. It wouldn't matter if I was in tenth grade!"

Addy took a large gulp and said in a choked voice, "He got so angry at me. He started calling me names and said he was going to say terrible things about me." Addy's eyes got all teary, and reluctantly, she started crying.

Skye and I hugged her. Then much to my astonishment, Skye stated angrily, "If that disgusting idiot says one nasty word about you, he'll be totally sorry! You just tell him that—or better still, I'll tell him myself! I won't let anyone treat my best friend like that."

I jumped in and added, "That goes for me too!"

Addy gave us a small grin and replied, "No one has ever been so lucky to have friends like you."

Skye replied with complete confidence, "You just let us know if there's any problem, and I mean *any problem*, and Leira and I will be there to help you 100 percent!"

I said, "I'm beginning to think of us as the Three Musketeers! 'All for one and one for all!'" Skye and Addy looked at me oddly. Tentatively I added, "Well, I think that's the right saying. But what I mean is, if we all stand together, then no one can hurt us, because we're an unbeatable team!" After a brief pause, I hesitantly asked, "Does that make sense?"

Addy smiled knowingly and responded, "Yeah, I get it." Skye nodded in agreement.

For a few moments, we walked along in silence, thinking about our day. We were nearing Grimly Manor, and all our attention shifted to it. Curiosity from the events of the sleepover crept into our minds.

Chapter 10
Discovery in the Cemetery

AS WE CONTINUED walking home, we soon passed by Grimly Manor. Skye glanced back at it and asked, "Hey, do you want to go over to the cemetery after we finish our homework and see if we can find any clues?"

I responded, "I'm not sure if our parents will allow us to visit the cemetery. There's no harm in asking though."

Skye said, "Well, my parents aren't home yet—only Liam will be there—so I could just tell him I'm going to do my homework over your house, Leira."

Addy grimaced and said, "I'll find out from my mom if it's OK to do my homework at your house too. Then I'll ask about the cemetery, but I have a feeling that she's going to say no. She's already told me that she doesn't want me going near Grimly Manor until she has talked to more people in the neighborhood about it. At the very least, I think we should be able to do our homework together."

We stopped at Addy's house first. Skye and I waited outside. After asking her mother if she could do her homework at my house, her mom replied, "All right, but be home by five thirty for tacos."

Addy responded with a huge grin, saying, "I won't be late!" I knew tacos were Addy's favorite food. Then I heard Addy casually ask, "Mom, when we're finished with our homework, can Leira, Skye, and I go over to the cemetery and look at the old headstones? I've heard the oldest ones have some really unique carvings on them."

Silence filled the air for a moment, and then we heard Mrs. Davies reply, "I don't like the idea of you going near that place until I've learned more about the owner of Grimly Manor."

We heard Addy pleading, "But, Mom, both Leira and Skye will be with me, and we'll only be looking at the headstones. We promise not to go anywhere near the manor." Addy begged one more time, "Please…"

When she came out of her house, she said dismally, as we had already heard, "Well, I can go over your house to do homework, Leira, but I can't go to the cemetery."

Skye asked disappointedly, "What's the problem? It's only a cemetery. Maybe Leira and I should talk to your mom."

Addy responded defensively, "My mom wants to know more about Mr. Grimly, and I'm absolutely sure that if you guys talked to her, it would just make her angry."

Skye apologized, "I'm sorry, Addy. That was a stupid idea."

Addy gave Skye a generous hug and replied, "That's all right. My mom's decision really upset me too. I don't see any problem taking a quick walk through the cemetery during the day."

Listening to the conversation, I interrupted in a slightly sneaky tone, "Hey, we could just quickly go over there after our homework is finished. We won't be there very long, and we'll be back before you have to be home. What do you think?"

Skye raised an eyebrow and exclaimed softly in astonishment, "I can't believe that you would suggest that! That's something I would have come up with."

Skye and I looked at Addy in expectation. She glanced from one of us to the other and, with a slight frown, tentatively replied, "Well, I don't think it will hurt to have a quick look around—will it?"

I replied, "Addy, I'm not as fearless as Skye, but I think that in broad daylight, entering a town cemetery won't put us in any danger. But I would definitely understand if you don't want to go. And if you don't, then I think we should call off the whole thing for now."

Skye challenged me, "You've got to be kidding! We stayed up almost all night watching for something to happen! We know he—or whoever—was in the cemetery two nights ago. Don't you want to see why? If we wait much longer, any clues he left might be gone!"

I thought about it and finally replied, "You're absolutely right, Skye. We shouldn't take a chance on letting any possible clues disappear. Let's investigate it right now, as quickly as possible. Addy, you can stay at my house while we're gone."

Addy said heatedly, "Well, if you're both going, then I'm going too. I'm one-third of this team, and I certainly don't see anything wrong with visiting a public cemetery. But we'll have to be extra careful because of Josie. She might see us walking there and come after us—or worse, she might tell my mom."

Skye and I were both astounded by Addy's statement, but we agreed and headed across the street so Skye could stop at her house and check in with Liam. He was busy working on a school project when Skye interrupted him, and said, "I'm going over Leira's house. I'll call Mom after she gets home."

Liam snapped at her, "I'm working on important school stuff! I don't care where you're going, just as long as it's away from here!"

Skye replied, "No problem. I'm leaving now."

We arrived at my house and completed our homework in record time. Then I went and found my dad getting ready to take Lucky for a walk. He'd gotten off work early that day. I simply asked, "Dad, is it all right if Skye, Addy, and I take a walk over to the old cemetery? We're interested in trying to decipher the old inscriptions on the tombstones. We won't be long because Addy has to be home by five thirty for dinner."

My dad looked at me inquisitively and asked, "Since when are you so interested in reading old headstones?"

I replied, "Well, Aunt Debbie does quite a lot of genealogy, and she said that if we couldn't read the stones, there's a way to take paper and trace them or something like that. The three of us are going to try and find one that the inscription looks interesting but we can't read the whole thing. Then I'll find out from Aunt Debbie about how to finish it."

Dad replied, "OK, but instead of taking Lucky to the hollow for a walk, I'll just take her around the block so I can check on how you're doing."

Grinning, I replied, "Thanks, Dad! We won't be gone long, though, so you'd better hurry up."

We started out from my house, but unfortunately, Josie was playing in Addy's front yard, so we snuck out cautiously through her backyard. Then we got stuck because old Mrs. Crimpton, who lived next to Addy, had a high picket fence surrounding her backyard. We crept along the side of Addy's house and peeked around the corner. Josie was still playing with their little dog, Shaggy. The three of us waited impatiently for her to go inside. It was almost four thirty, and time seemed to be rushing by. Less than ten minutes later, we heard Mrs. Davies calling Josie into the house. We were so relieved.

As we hurried down to the end of the street and entered the graveyard by the only public entrance, we glanced behind us to make sure no one was watching, including Josie. I opened the rusty gate that led into the cemetery. As we began wandering through the grass strewn with October leaves, I wondered if we would find any clue to the swinging light we had seen. I started to feel a bit spooked because Halloween was almost upon us. Several homes in our neighborhood had scary decorations put up. While walking through the graveyard, I inhaled the beautiful but strangely sad aroma of the moist rotting leaves. It had always been fun to rake a big pile of leaves and jump into them, but not here. As we kicked our way along through the leaves, I glanced over my shoulder, seeing the back of Grimly Manor for the first time. It seemed even more terrifying than it had from the street. I tapped both Skye and Addy on their shoulders and nodded toward the back of the manor. Then I asked in a whisper, "Don't you think it's even creepier seeing it from here—in the cemetery?"

Skye suddenly cried out, "Look at that!"

Addy and I both jumped out of our skins, and I blurted out in fright, "What is it?"

Skye pointed and excitedly stated, "Over there! There's a bunch of new flowers laid out on that tombstone. Come on, let's check out that grave."

Addy tentatively said, "It's near the middle of the cemetery. Are you sure we have enough time?" I looked at my watch and assured her that it was only five o'clock so we had enough time to quickly go over, check it out, and then head back home.

As we neared the gravestone, the three of us became extremely uneasy. We walked up close enough to read the inscription. All the while, I kept glancing over my shoulder because I felt like someone was watching us. Maybe someone was.

Addy read the inscription aloud. "Here lie two loving parents. Esther May Grimly, born May 2, 1910, and Elijah Grimly, born January 18, 1908. They both lovingly gave up their lives on October 21, 1945." Addy looked at both of us and, with a horrified expression, said, "October 21, that was yesterday!"

Just then, from behind one of the tombstones, a cat jumped out hissing! The three of us screamed in fright, until I got a better look at her. Then with my nerves under control, I breathed a sigh of relief and said, "It's OK, you guys, it's just my cat, Emmy. But I think that's enough for today. Let's get out of here."

As we left the cemetery, I noticed my dad several houses away and heading in our direction. I waved at him, and he returned the wave. I had forgotten to tell Addy and Skye that Dad was keeping an eye on us. Actually, during all the excitement, I'd forgotten too.

As we hurried back home, I asked my friends, "Wasn't it about forty-five minutes after midnight when we saw the light in the graveyard?" When they both nodded, I continued, "Well, if it was twelve forty-five in the morning, then that means it was October 21, so… he must have been putting the flowers on the grave because they're his parents and that's the day they died."

Both Skye and Addy excitedly agreed. After a moment or two, Skye added enthusiastically, "So we actually saw Mr. *Grimly* that night. Wow!"

I scratched my head in disbelief and said, "The three of us are the first people to have ever seen him outside since he returned to his home. Oh my gosh, that's so amazing! Unfortunately, it's getting late, so we'd better get home and talk about it tomorrow."

We arrived at Addy's house just in time, but awaiting us on the front lawn was a sight that didn't bode well. It was Josie. In a haughty tone, she taunted, "You're in trouble! You're in trouble! I saw you coming out of the cemetery." We looked at each other worriedly. Stupidly, we had forgotten to sneak back secretly because we'd been completely astonished by what we had found. Addy took a deep breath and said, "I'll see you tomorrow—I hope."

Chapter 11
The Thirtieth of October

ON TUESDAY MORNING, when Skye, Addy, and I started walking to school, I asked, "What happened? Did you get in trouble?"

Addy, with her eyes downcast, replied, "Absolutely. I'm grounded for a whole week. I can't come over or even call you! Can you believe it? The only good thing is that it ends on Halloween, so at least I'll still get to go trick-or-treating."

Trying to sound cheerful, I replied, "Well, that's something to look forward to. Just don't forget to watch Grimly Manor because any time now the house should be decorated. If either of you wakes up during the night, be sure to check out if anything is happening. OK?" Skye and Addy both nodded in agreement. Then I stated enthusiastically, "I'm so excited! I can't wait until Halloween when we'll knock on his door again."

Skye looked at me with a raised eyebrow and asked sarcastically, "You're going to knock on the door, and you're excited about it?"

Avoiding Skye's eyes and chewing on my lower lip, I replied quietly, "Well, we're all going to knock on the door together. Aren't we?"

Skye said, "Well, that's comforting. But if either of you steps back again, I'm going to be really angry!"

Addy and I glanced at each other, then back at Skye, and I responded, "Don't worry, we won't." Addy nodded in agreement.

The week trickled by. None of us saw anything unusual happening during the night. But then again, we didn't usually wake up until the alarm went off. But on the thirtieth of October, when I looked out the window, there it was! The whole manor and its surrounding property had the most fascinating and frightening decorations I had ever seen!

I phoned Skye immediately, and when she answered, I excitedly asked, "Have you seen Grimly Manor this morning?"

Skye sleepily replied, "No, I just woke up."

I urged, "Well, hurry up and look out your window!"

Taking the phone with her, Skye quickly crossed her room, looked out her side window, and yelled into the phone, "Unbelievable! That's amazing. Let's get dressed and go have a closer look."

I anxiously replied, "I'll meet you outside in about fifteen minutes." Skye interrupted and quickly asked, "Wait, did you phone Addy?"

I responded, "No, remember, she's still grounded until tomorrow."

Skye replied, "Oh yeah, I forgot. That's a bummer. Anyway, I'll meet you outside in fifteen minutes."

We met in front of Skye's house shortly after. With our nerves on edge, we slowly walked toward the manor. The nearer we got, the more we became entranced by the decorations. The first things visible were the propped-up coffins with realistic skeletons placed in them. They were really creepy.

I asked Skye, "Remember that rumor about Mr. Grimly digging up some graves? What if…" I left the sentence unfinished.

In a slightly aggravated tone, Skye asked, "Leira, are you talking about the rumor spread by Frankie? You've already explained why he probably said it, so why are you mentioning it now?"

"Well," I replied, "those skeletons look awful real to me. Don't you think so?"

Skye scoffed at me, "With all the scary movies I've seen, I'd say they're terrific replicas."

Gazing around, we saw at least a hundred carved pumpkins. Most of them had terrifying faces carved on them, although some were quite funny. Positioned around the yard were several cornstalks, with those strange-looking gourds surrounding the bases. There were bats and ghosts suspended from quite a few trees flying in the breeze. I had observed previous Halloween decorations throughout the years, but this definitely topped anything I'd seen before. Hesitantly, I said to

Skye, "I can't wait for tonight to see how it lights up, and especially for tomorrow night—Halloween."

Skye immediately grinned and replied, "Yeah, me too. It's going to be awesome, and hopefully we'll find out something new about Mr. Grimly." I said, "I don't know about that, but I'm definitely not looking forward to walking by those coffins."

We hurried back home and grabbed our backpacks. At least Addy would be able to see the house while we were walking to school.

That evening, Skye came over to help me clean out my pumpkin. It was *enormous!* According to my parents and teachers, I'm a good artist, so one of my favorite parts of making our pumpkin has always been drawing the face.

Skye willingly helped scrape the slimy insides out and then asked, "Can we pick out the seeds and toast them?"

I shouted, "Mom!"

She walked into the dining room with several bags of candy and asked, "What do you need?"

I asked, "If Skye and I pick out the pumpkin seeds, would you bake them for us?"

She looked at me skeptically and asked, "Are *you* actually going to pick out the seeds?" She knew I hated that slimy goop.

I answered, "Well, of course I'm going to help—at least a little bit."

Mom replied wearily, "All right, tell me when you're ready."

As Skye and I relentlessly continued our gooey work, my mom lit our Halloween candle. I just love the aroma. It smells exactly like candy corns! It definitely helps set the mood for Halloween.

Just then, the phone rang. It was elderly Mrs. Crimpton, who lived right next door to Addy. My mother spoke to her in what sounded like a concerned voice.

As my mom left the room with the phone, I quietly said to Skye, "Mrs. Crimpton is the nosiest busybody in the neighborhood. She's too old to leave her house much, but she definitely enjoys gossiping. I bet something really interesting is happening right now."

My mom walked back into the room with a worried look on her face and stated, "Apparently, we have some nasty kids roaming the streets tonight because it's Cabbage Night. Mrs. Crimpton declared she's had several phone calls from neighbors."

Skye interrupted and asked, "What the heck is Cabbage Night?"

Observing her surprised looks, my mom replied, "Cabbage Night is a ridiculous tradition where pranks are played on other families—mostly people you don't like."

Skye inquired, "What kind of pranks?"

My mother replied, "Kids do stupid or silly things on Cabbage Night. Some take pumpkins or smash them. Others throw eggs at cars or homes, and a few even drape toilet paper over the trees or bushes. Those are the most common things that happen. Tonight, apparently, some annoying kids are smashing pumpkins, throwing eggs, and stealing decorations. So for now, do not go out of the house. If you want to help, when you finish carving your pumpkin, be on the lookout from the front window until Skye goes home. Oh! I almost forgot—when the seeds are ready to bake, just let me know, and while they're toasting, I'll make some hot apple cider to go with them. One more thing—when Skye is ready to go home, I'll walk with her."

I said, "Mom, she just has to walk across the street."

She promptly replied, "Better safe than sorry."

I replied, "All right, but I have a special favor to ask. Can I please carve the pumpkin this year? Please?"

Mom replied apprehensively, "All right. I'll go get the carving knife, but be very careful!" When she returned from my dad's workroom, she handed me the carver. She discreetly withdrew, but just enough to keep a close watch on me for about five minutes.

After my mom had left the room, Skye said, "I can stay until eight o'clock, and it's only six now. That gives us plenty of time to watch for those troublemakers!"

As my stomach grumbled, I replied, "Yeah, and we can munch on the pumpkin seeds and drink my mom's yummy apple cider while we're watching."

Carefully, I finished carving the pumpkin (which I named Seedie) and stood back with a critical eye to survey my work. It wasn't too bad.

Skye said proudly, "You did an awesome job!"

When the pumpkin and its seeds were ready, I shouted for my mom. When she entered the room, I shouted with raised arms and said, "TA-DA! Could you please get a candle and take pictures of my masterpiece?"

Mom smiled at me and replied, "You've certainly done a terrific job! It's much, much better than I could have done! I'll get the camera and turn the oven on."

After the oven was hot and my mom had taken a bunch of pictures (which included several funny ones with Skye and me in them), my mother toasted up the best batch of pumpkin seeds I had ever tasted! With our mugs of hot apple cider and our plate full of pumpkin seeds, we moved into the living room to watch for the troublemakers.

My father had placed a few small pumpkins and a couple of other inexpensive decorations near the road just to tempt the hooligans. He and Mom had already told us that they would bring in the stuff before they went to bed. Mom and Dad were watching TV as Skye and I sat in the dark, gazing out the front window. While munching on our salty pumpkin seeds and sipping the savory apple cider, we watched for any strange happenings, and not only near us—occasionally our eyes drifted toward Grimly Manor.

Skye had to be home in an hour. After almost half an hour had gone by, Skye unexpectedly pressed her face close to the glass, squinted, and whispered, "Did you see something move?"

I quickly responded, "No. Where?"

Skye pointed across the street slightly to the right of her house. As I spotted the movement, we both watched intently and followed it (or them) creeping slowly away from Skye's house and across the next two houses on the street. Both of us saw some movement in the bushes surrounding the home of the Waltons.

Skye burst out, "Quick! Get your parents!"

Racing from the living room, I yelled over my shoulder, "Whatever you do, don't lose sight of them!"

I returned quickly with Mom and Dad in tow. Mom had her cell phone, and we watched expectantly while she called the police. Suddenly, we saw them again! Two people wearing dark clothes, throwing pumpkins into the street, and then racing toward the next house!

My mother talked to the police, explaining what was happening. As she hung up the phone, she said, "The police are on the way, and they're only three blocks from us, so they'll be here shortly!"

The officers drove up silently to where my mom had instructed them. With bated breath, we saw two cruisers (with their lights off) carefully surround the suspects. Without hesitation, the police jumped out of their vehicles, raced after them, and captured them quickly! It was so exciting to think that we had helped them. Hopefully, there wouldn't be any more mischief that night.

Skye and I continued to sit in the dark for a while after Mom and Dad offered their congratulations. When they finally left the room, I commented to Skye, "Boy, if that happened tonight, I wonder what will occur tomorrow night on Halloween?"

Skye looked at me with wide eyes and replied, "Well, we only have twenty-four hours until we know."

Shortly after that, my mother came back into the living room and said, "Skye, I'll walk you home now."

Chapter 12
Halloween!

HALLOWEEN HAD FINALLY arrived. That day at school seemed to drag on forever. The only fun part about it was that the kindergarten students got to wear their costumes all day, and they paraded through every class. One was dressed up as Darth Vader from *Star Wars*!

Walking home after school, I asked Addy, "Did Jeffrey say anything to you today?"

She answered angrily, "Yes, he most certainly did. He declared that he was going to throw rotten eggs at my house tonight unless I agreed to go out with him! Do you believe the nerve of that kid? He's the most horrible person I've ever known!"

Outraged, Skye snapped, "I can't believe it! Didn't you tell him what I said? I'm going to have a talk with that idiot."

Addy responded, "Actually, Skye, I didn't have the courage to tell him what you said. I'm sorry, but I was kind of hoping he'd just leave me alone. Besides, I'm pretty sure that he doesn't know where I live."

I interrupted and asked, "What time do you want to get together tonight to go trick-or-treating, and whose house do you want to start at?"

We talked about it for a while and decided to meet at my house, but first, we needed to get our parents' approval. As we passed Grimly Manor, Skye asked with a smirk, "Are both of you ready to go trick-or-treating there?"

Skye had that gleam in her eye that said, "I dare you."

Addy and I both replied without hesitation, "Of course!" Then I added, "And we promise not to step backward like last time."

Addy glanced toward me with a slightly fearful look but replied with a false smile, "Right!"

After we arrived home, we each spoke to our parents. They finally agreed that we could go trick-or-treating together without a parent, but we had to stop in after each of the five streets in our neighborhood. We decided to meet at my house at six o'clock; it would be dark by then. Our parents said we had to be finished by eight o'clock. Considering the number of streets, I thought we had enough time to make it through all of them. In the back of my mind, I wondered if we'd really have the courage to return to Grimly Manor, and if we did, I was worried and a little excited about what would happen.

Skye came early, about five forty-five. She looked fantastic but silly. She was dressed up in baby pajamas and carrying a pacifier and a baby bottle. She had little teardrops and big rosy cheeks painted on her face. She also carried a large pillowcase, on which she had creatively written "Diaper Change." She had pulled up her shiny nut-brown hair into a bun and wore an elastic baby cap over it.

I said, "You look terrific. What a great idea!"

She looked closely at my costume and replied, "Your outfit is awesome too!"

I was dressed as an army lady, with an extra ladylike look. My costume was camouflage pants and a shirt with black fluffy material at the bottom of the cuffs and sleeves. It also had an extremely cute hat trimmed with fluffy black feathery stuff. I could have worn my dad's real army hat, but it was way too large and very heavy. Plus it wasn't nearly as pretty!

Finally, Addy arrived. She had kept her costume a secret. We both laughed hysterically when we saw her. She was dressed up as a huge jar of mustard!

I burst out, "Addy! You hate mustard. What on earth made you decide on that Halloween costume?"

Reluctantly, Addy responded, "Well, we didn't get to the party store until last night because of my being grounded, so my choices were extremely limited. Would you rather I'd have been an oversized pickle? They didn't have ketchup in my size!"

We laughed again, and I declared, "I'd rather you were a pickle because I can't stand mustard either."

Skye promptly replied, "Well, I love mustard, so don't worry. You'll definitely give everyone a good laugh, and besides, no one will know who you actually are."

Addy paused for a moment then said with a giggle, "My sister, Josie, is dressed up as ketchup, so I guess people might figure out we're related."

I added, "You'd better warn Josie to stay out of my sight, because if there's one thing I love, it's ketchup!"

With the three of us laughing uncontrollably, we set out trick-or-treating.

After we had completed the first three streets, our bags were full. When we checked in at Skye's house, we emptied our bags into large plastic ones to pick up later and continued on to the fourth street, which was very close to Grimly Manor.

As we left the house three homes away from the manor, an adorable fluffy dog raced up to us. At first, we were scared because we had never seen it before. But the dog just jumped up, licked us, and barked. She was mostly cream-colored, with a couple of brown splashes here and there. She was a small-to medium-sized dog and very pudgy. It was obvious that she could knock us over with her enthusiasm if she wanted to.

Addy cooed, "Oh, are you lost, sweetie?" Then she bent forward and began scratching the dog's neck. It was then that she spotted a tag on the collar and said to the dog, "Let's take a look at your tag and see if we can figure out where you belong."

As Addy gazed at the brilliant silver tag on the leather collar, she gasped. Glancing fearfully up at us, she said, "The name on the tag says the owner is Albert Grimly!"

We looked apprehensively at one another, and I stated, "Well, the only thing to do is take her back to Grimly Manor. We were planning to go there anyway."

Everyone agreed, and the three of us set off for the manor, skipping the houses in between. Skye was carrying the dog, and after holding her for a while, she shifted the dog's position and said, "She's a lot heavier than I thought she was."

I asked Skye, "Do you want me to hold her?"

Skye replied, "No, we're almost there, but thanks for asking."

As we neared Grimly Manor, we saw in detail all the decorations that had been set up. It was so creepy! As we got nearer the coffins with the skeletons in them, we saw that they had blotches of goopy stuff hanging from different parts of their bodies and hair dangled sparsely from their heads. The ghosts and bats were very realistic up close. There was a fake graveyard set up on the front lawn, and when we passed by it, a skeletal hand poked up through the ground! We could hear eerie music that seemed to come from every direction. Every now and then, when we stepped on one of the slate stones along the pathway, a shrill scream would rip through the air. I imagined that there must be some sort of thing underneath the stones that set off the screams. I'd never seen or heard anything like it before.

Trying to ignore our fears, we finally reached the rickety front door. At that crucial instant, we looked at each other, and I said with a trembling voice, "On the count of three, we'll knock firmly on the door twice. Agreed?"

Skye and Addy both nodded. Skye took a deep breath and said, "One, two, three!"

We banged hard on the door twice. Just then, the dog started squirming so much that she escaped from Skye's arms. She immediately began yapping happily and jumping up at the front door. When it opened, we gasped in shock! Staring at us from inside was a werewolf! The dog leapt directly at it, sending it flailing to the floor!

We gazed in intense horror for a moment before quickly turning and fleeing in fright. Then unexpectedly, we heard a loud voice yelling after us. "Come back! It's only a costume. Please, I want to thank you for finding my dog."

Hesitantly, we stopped and slowly returned. We stood on the steps as far back from the door as possible. We were too afraid to get any closer because the man wouldn't take off his horrible mask. The werewolf said to us, "My dog's name is Puffin, and I love her tremendously. Someone cut a hole in my back fence yesterday, and she escaped sometime during the night."

He continued with deep concern, "She's escaped only once before, a couple of months ago. The dog warden found her for me two days later. I was completely lost without her during that time. I can't thank you enough for finding her and bringing her home. Would you like to come inside? I'd like to give you a reward for your efforts."

We were all still terrified, but I bravely stuttered, "No thanks, that's… um… quite all right. We have to get going now because our parents are waiting for us."

The werewolf said, "By the way, if you don't already know, I'm Albert Grimly."

I replied, "Yes, we thought you were. That's how we figured out where to bring Puffin."

Thanking us again, he dropped a big scoop of candy into each of our bags. He said, "I sincerely hope you will come back on occasion to visit Puffin. She loves children."

We promptly responded, "Thank you!" and then ran off toward home.

While running, I said breathlessly, "Let's get together first thing tomorrow and talk about what happened."

Then Addy stopped and shouted, "Wait!"

Skye and I stopped abruptly, and I asked anxiously, "What is it?"

Addy responded with a fearful question. "Do you think it's safe to eat his candy?"

I breathed a sigh of relief, shrugged my shoulders, and replied, "I haven't the slightest idea. Let's just leave that up to our parents."

It had been a Halloween that we would never forget! Nothing would ever top that—or could it?

Chapter 13
A Birthday Present

NOVEMBER 4 WAS Skye's twelfth birthday. She didn't know it, but there was going to be a surprise party at her house. Everyone arrived by five o'clock in the afternoon, while Skye's mother took her out to buy a new winter coat. Seven girls were invited, and we planned to hide in the living room behind the chairs and sofa. Addy and I had helped Mr. Finnegan decorate the room with balloons and banners while Skye and Mrs. Finnegan were out shopping. Near the fireplace, we arranged the pile of presents from the guests. As Skye's mother pulled into the driveway, we hunched down and tried not to giggle.

When Skye and her mom entered the house, we heard her mother say in a disheartened voice, "Skye, I'm sorry we couldn't do more for your birthday, but there is one more present from Daddy, Liam, and me in the living room. I hope you like it."

When Skye entered the living room, Liam flicked on the lights. Then everyone popped up, yelling, "SURPRISE!"

Skye appeared stunned! With a deep blush spreading across her face, she gasped, "WOW! I don't believe this! How did everyone keep this a secret from me?"

We laughed and raced to her, giving her an enormous hug. Surprisingly, I actually saw a few tears in her eyes.

We had a terrific time! We played Truth or Dare and Scene It?, which was a DVD game we all enjoyed. For a while, we played some music and danced. Skye had a microphone, and those of us with enough nerve sang a little karaoke. Finally, we had pizza, cake, and ice cream. The cake was soooo adorable. The bakery had shaped and decorated it like a ladybug. Next, Skye opened her presents. Most of the girls had gotten her jewelry, stuffed animals, bath stuff, and some cool clothes. Liam's gift proved to be quite different. Skye opened the present tentatively. While looking at her elder brother, she suspiciously inquired, "Liam, is this going to be another one of your prankster gifts?"

He instantly replied in a serious voice, "No, Mom even approved of it."

Skye glanced at her mom, who nodded her head and smiled. Skye unwrapped the gift, which turned out to be a beautiful enameled music box. It had a luminous unicorn painted on the top, and inside the box was a breathtaking miniature unicorn statuette.

Liam hurriedly urged, "Well, wind it up!"

After Skye wound it, the unicorn began rotating slowly to the sound of soothing classical music. Liam then mentioned, "It plays two songs, but you have to push the button on the side to change it."

Skye pushed the button, and all of a sudden, a multicolored substance squirted out, right from the center of the box! It sprayed Skye's face and shirt. Skye screamed, and all of us backed away as quickly as possible because the stuff had an awful odor.

Skye's father pushed his way through, seized Liam's arm, and hurriedly dragged him from the room. Skye's mother cried out in horror, "Skye, I'm so terribly sorry. I didn't know anything about a second button. Come on, let's get you cleaned up, and then you can open your present from Daddy and me." Skye stood up and followed her mom out of the room. She never uttered a sound.

While Skye was gone, I said to Addy, "She's told me a few things about Liam, but I didn't realize what she has gone through until now. He's an absolute nightmare."

Katie, one of the girls from our class, added, "I hope he gets exactly what he deserves!"

Addy shook her head in disbelief and said, "I always thought my little sister was horrible, but she's an angel compared to him."

In time, Skye returned. We were slightly puzzled because she had an enormous grin on her face.

I asked, "Skye, how can you possibly be so cheerful after what Liam did?"

Skye laughed and replied, "Because Dad made Liam hand over every last cent he has, and he's taking him down to the mall to buy me an iPod!"

We gasped in awe!

She added, "Not only that, but he's grounded for a month, and during that month, he has to do all my chores! It's about time they cracked down on him." Then she performed a little dance, singing, "I'm getting an iPod, I'm getting an iPod."

Everyone was laughing hard when Skye's mom returned. We tried unsuccessfully to stop. Her mom understood and said, "That's all right." Then she glanced over at Skye and asked, "Aren't you going to open your last present now?"

Skye quickly opened her parents' gift, and when she figured out what it was, a sneaky smile spread over her face. It was an excellent pair of binoculars! Addy, Skye, and I glanced at each other with looks of excitement. Now we had the ability to see more clearly what was happening at Grimly Manor!

After that, we figured the party was over, and we would have to lay out our stuff in the living room for our sleepover. But Skye's mom said, "Follow me, I have a surprise for you!" She guided us up the stairs to the second floor.

Skye questioned worriedly, "Mom, are we *all* going to sleep in my bedroom? I think it's just a little too small."

Her mother replied with a sneaky voice, "Just follow me."

When we reached the second floor, Mrs. Finnegan led us down a hallway and opened what seemed to be a closet door, but it wasn't! There were stairs inside and while climbing them, I realized what the stairs led to! I whispered to Addy, "This leads to the turret tower."

Addy responded with a grimace, "I think it's kind of creepy."

When we arrived at the top, we all gasped! It was totally amazing!

Her mother had put up two sets of bunk beds and four sleeping bags on blow-up mattresses. Skye turned around and exclaimed, "Mom, how did you do all this without me knowing? This is unbelievable!"

Her mom replied, "Well, it wasn't easy, but it certainly was worth it!" Crossing the room, Mrs. Finnegan pointed out a mini fridge with sodas and a cabinet full of snacks. Then she proceeded to say, "And… if you hadn't noticed, there's a big-screen TV/DVD player with all your favorite movies! Happy birthday! I love you!"

I could tell Skye was completely overwhelmed but managed to say without bursting into tears, "Thanks, Mom. Thanks for the best birthday ever." She ran over and gave her mom an enormous hug!

Her mother then added, "I have only one thing left to say to everyone, and you need to take it seriously, *all* of you! Do *not* go up into the attic of the turret. It's not safe, so don't even think about it!" Skye nodded, and everyone peered around the room to figure out where the opening to the attic was. Just then, Skye raised her eyes to the northeast corner of the room, and we saw a small entrance panel in the ceiling with a cover over it. It was large enough for a bulky person to fit through, but there was no ladder.

Skye's mom added in a cheerful voice, "Well, good night, have fun and don't wake us up unless there's an emergency. Skye, don't forget to show everyone where the bathroom is, and if anyone gets homesick, there's a phone next to the TV. Good night!"

We checked out the movies her mother had left for us, and together we chose a thriller called *The Rose*. Most of us hadn't seen it, but Skye had, and she said, "It's the best spooky movie I've ever seen!" It was her birthday, so even though one or two of the girls weren't too excited about watching a horror movie, we all agreed to watch it for her sake.

Skye chose the bottom spot of one of the bunk beds and offered me the next choice. I chose the bunk on top of hers, and then Addy selected the top bunk of the other set. We settled down with snacks and drinks to watch the movie. By the time the movie ended, it was almost midnight. Some of the girls were a little scared, but they fell asleep quickly. I whispered to Addy, "I hope no one has scary dreams."

Addy replied with a question, "Are you talking about me?"

I answered, "No, I was speaking about the others."

Skye overheard us and asked, "Addy, are you afraid?"

Addy replied, "No, I'm perfectly fine! Let's just go to sleep."

Skye and I said together, "Night, night. Sweet dreams."

Several minutes later, as I lay awake, wondering about the attic room above us, I whispered to Skye, "Skye, are you still up?"

Skye whispered back, "Yeah."

I inquired, "Do you know why your mother doesn't want anyone going up into the attic of the turret?"

Skye replied, "I don't know. She said it isn't safe, so I guess there's something broken or whatever. Don't worry about it."

Skye then added, "Leira, by the way, I loved your present, and I love being here. This has been the greatest birthday I've ever had!"

I told her, "Skye, since you and Addy have arrived, I've been happier than I've ever thought possible. Sharing your birthday has just added to the joy! Night, night, and of course, sweet dreams."

Chapter 14
A Campout

THE FOLLOWING DAY was Saturday. Addy, Skye, and I got together in the afternoon to plan a sleepover at my house that night. I was sure I could talk my parents into it, but we wanted to sleep outdoors in the tent as well. We had been having very warm weather the last three days, which didn't happen often in the Northeast. So it all came down to three specific questions. First, would my parents agree to the sleepover? Second, could I possibly persuade my dad to set up the tent? And last of all, how would we be able to spy on Grimly Manor without getting caught?

While Skye and Addy waited in my bedroom, I ran downstairs to find my mom. As soon as I saw her, I decided to go for it. I danced toward her and cheerfully asked, "Mom, can Skye and Addy sleep over tonight so we can give Mrs. Finnegan a break after all the work she did for Skye's party? Oh, and one more thing, since it's so warm out, could we please sleep in the tent?"

My mother replied with a shrug, "Sure, you can have Skye and Addy sleep over, but you'll have to ask Dad about the tent. That's a lot of work, and even though the weather's good, I'm not certain Dad will have enough time to set it up."

The three of us went downstairs to the basement, where Dad was trying to fix an old lantern. With big eyes and pleading voices, we asked if there was anything we could do that would convince him to set up the tent in the backyard for a sleepover. My dad didn't ever say much, but when he did, it was either really funny or not a good thing.

As usual, my father took his time before replying, "Well, who's going to hammer in the first stake?"

We jumped up and down laughing and shouting, "YES!"

Then, I gave Dad a great big hug and said, "Dad, you're the best dad in the whole world! Thank you so much!"

Enthusiastically, we helped set everything up over the next three hours. It was exhausting work but well worth it. However, while blowing up the mattresses, I started feeling a little guilty about spying on Mr. Grimly and also a tiny bit nervous about what might happen.

Shortly after we ate dinner, my mom brought snacks and drinks out to the tent. Then we got into our sleeping bags and discussed our plans. I said, "Well, we don't want to get too close to the house, so I think if we just hide behind the bushes at the corner of the manor, we should be OK."

Skye suggested, "I think one of us should stay here in case your mother or father comes out to check on us."

Addy nodded in agreement and said, "One of us should stay, and every hour we could switch places. If one of your parents comes out, then whoever's here could say that the other two went back to one of their homes to get something they had forgotten. How does that sound?"

I exclaimed, "Addy, you're a genius! The first watch could be from nine until ten o'clock. I think I should stay here first as that's the most likely time one of my parents might come out to check on us. So at ten o'clock, Skye should come back, and we'll switch places. Does that sound good?" Skye and Addy nodded. It was eight thirty, so we still had until nine o'clock to think about any other details we might have missed.

Skye and Addy left the tent at nine o'clock with the new binoculars. They crept along the road, keeping to the shadows of the homes, trees, and shrubbery until they reached the edge of the manor property. Crouching down behind some bushes, they took turns parting them and peering through. They watched in anticipation and nervousness for something to occur.

Addy whispered to Skye, "I'm not really sure that I want something to happen. I've got the creeps already. Do you think we'll have to keep this up all night?"

Skye replied in exasperation, "I don't know. I thought this was what we were waiting for. Aren't you even a bit excited that we might find out something important?"

Addy responded, "Well, I guess so. I'm just relieved that we don't have to get any closer than this."

At ten o'clock, Skye left Addy to switch places with me. Addy wasn't very eager to be left alone, even for five minutes. I ran as fast as I could to the bushes where she was hiding, and it was obvious that she was glad that I had hurried. I breathlessly asked, "Have you seen anything happen yet?"

She replied, "No, we've seen some movement in the house but nothing really strange."

While gazing through the bushes, we heard the sound of a vehicle approaching. I quickly turned to Addy and exclaimed, "Duck down!" We burrowed ourselves even further into the prickly bushes.

Addy emitted a painful "Ouch! That's my hand you're stepping on."

I apologized, and then we both tried to see what had happened to the vehicle we heard. Banging our heads together while trying to peer through the bushes, I gasped, "Look! It's some kind of truck, and it's pulling into Mr. Grimly's driveway. Can you see it?"

Addy replied in an aggravated tone, "No, not with your hair dangling in my face!"

"Oops!" I replied in embarrassment. "I'm sorry about that." I untangled my hair from the bushes, pulled it back, and moved over a little, hoping Addy could see better. Then, I asked her again, "Can you see the truck now?"

Addy stated, "I see it, and there's a person stepping down from the truck. I can't tell if it's a man or a woman. Give me the binoculars."

I replied, "Hey, this was my idea, just give me a couple of minutes to look first. Move over a little please. How come you're so grumpy tonight anyway? This is exactly what we've been waiting for!"

Addy replied, "I'm sorry, Leira, but I'm tired, a bit chilly, scared, and my hand hurts. But never mind that. Just tell me what's happening."

I responded, "He's unloading some bags and placing them outside the back door. They might be grocery bags. I think he's finished now because he just closed the sliding door on the truck. Apparently, he's delivered several bags of groceries. At least I think they're groceries. Now he's pulling out some kind of envelope or paper from the doorway. Here, you take a look."

Addy grabbed the binoculars and nudged me over a little so she had a better view. She said in disappointment, "He's getting back into the truck. I missed everything!" At that point, we heard the truck's engine start up.

I tried to calm her by saying, "Maybe not everything. Do you notice anything written on the truck?"

Addy replied, "I think there might be, but the truck's hidden in the shadows. Wait, the truck's backing out, and there's a streetlight there. Hold on a minute. Yes!" she shouted out. "The writing says, 'Groceries Galore! Whatever you need, we deliver!'" We both smiled happily as we watched the truck drive away.

Meanwhile, as Addy and I were solving a piece of the mystery, Skye was waiting in the tent patiently. At approximately ten thirty, she noticed a shadowy light approaching. Skye was slightly nervous when the doorway to the tent unzipped, revealing *my mom!* She was holding a plate full of fresh home-baked brownies. Glancing quickly around the tent, she asked in concern, "Where are Addy and Leira?"

Skye gazed at her in dread and stuttered out, "Um… well… they went over to Addy's a few minutes ago because Addy forgot her favorite stuffed animal."

My mother looked at her in disbelief and said a bit tersely, "Well, here are some brownies that just came out of the oven. When Leira and Addy get back, please tell Leira I'd like to see her right away!" After my mom returned to the house, Skye ran as fast as she possibly could to reach me! When she arrived, we had a great deal to tell her! Unfortunately, first, we had to race back home and straighten everything out with my mom.

I immediately went inside the house to speak with my mother, while Addy began filling Skye in on what had occurred at Grimly Manor. My mother angrily stated, "Leira Jean MacGregor, I'm extremely upset with your behavior! You should have told me Addy needed to go back home for whatever she forgot. What if something had happened to any of you? Addy's parents must think terrible things about us. I didn't even call to let them know you were coming. And another thing, look at the time! Were her parents sleeping? Were they upset? I'm so disappointed in you. But we'll discuss this further in the morning. The last thing I'm going to say to you tonight is that you're grounded for a week starting tomorrow. Now go see your friends."

I replied guiltily, "I'm so sorry, Mom. I really didn't mean to let you down. We never ended up going into Addy's house, so her parents don't know, if that's any help. I promise I'll never do that again. Please forgive me?" Tears flowed down my cheeks.

Despite her anger, my mother gave me a hug and said, "I forgive you, but in addition to being grounded, you can spend your free time helping me clean the house!"

With a grimace, I responded, "OK."

While I was being chastised, Addy told Skye what we had seen, thanks to the use of her new binoculars. When Addy finished, she asked Skye, "Isn't that awesome? Aren't you excited about what we found out?"

Skye answered, "Yeah, but right now I'm more worried about Leira. Do you think she's in real trouble?"

Just then, Addy spotted the plateful of goodies and squealed, "Oh, this is fantastic! I love Mrs. MacGregor's homemade brownies!"

Skye sarcastically replied, "If it hadn't been for those brownies, we never would have been caught. And since you can't reply to my question with a mouthful of brownies, I'll answer it myself. I think Leira's in big trouble."

When I finally returned to the tent, Skye and Addy looked at me sympathetically and apprehensively. Skye asked, "How bad is it?"

Resigned to my punishment, I answered, "Well, I'm grounded for a week, but I deserve it. I really let my mother down."

It was obvious that Skye felt really bad for me as she tried to cheer me up by saying, "But at least you figured out a piece of the mystery! Addy told me what happened at the manor tonight. So now we know how he gets his food, even though we haven't any idea how he keeps it fresh without a refrigerator! Let's have some brownies and try to figure that out."

I reacted a bit annoyed, "It wasn't just *me* that found that out! Addy read the writing on the truck, and she couldn't have done it without your binoculars! Remember, we're a team!"

"Sorry—I didn't mean to bring down your spirits." Putting a forced smile on my face, I said, "Quick! Eat up or I'll get them all to myself!"

Skye and Addy each grabbed a brownie, but somehow, I wasn't hungry.

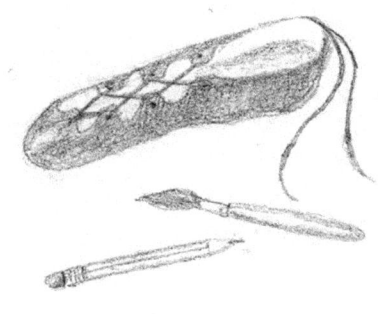

Chapter 15
A Long but Memorable Week

MY WEEK OF being grounded passed very slowly. As Monday proved to be another warm day, the three of us were able to walk to school together. When I met up with Skye and Addy, Skye asked, "Did anything worse happen to you than being grounded?"

I replied, "Not really, except that I'm not allowed to watch TV or use the computer, and I have to do extra chores."

Addy exclaimed, "That's awful! What did you end up doing with all that time?"

I shrugged my shoulders and told her, "I finished reading my book, which I had to do anyway because our book report is due Friday. Then I did all my chores. I also cleaned out my closet, which made my mom happy. Finally, last night, I lay awake in bed thinking about Mr. Grimly and wondering how we might be able to help him."

Skye, looking perplexed, asked, "What do you mean 'help him'? How can we possibly help him?"

I replied, "I'm not exactly sure, but don't you think he's probably lonely? All he appears to have is Puffin, and the holidays are almost here. I've never seen anyone else go over there."

Skye and Addy considered this for a moment, and then Addy changed the subject by saying, "At least we don't have reading buddies at school today!"

Skye and I both grimaced at her, and I replied, "Well, *you* don't! But we do, and I have the absolute worst reading buddy in history!"

Skye challenged, "I don't know about that, Leira! I definitely think my reading buddy is much worse than yours!"

Skye and I looked at each other and finally agreed that we both probably had the most disgusting and irritating second graders in the whole school.

I complained to Addy, "Hey, we're getting off the subject! I want to know if either of you are concerned about Mr. Grimly. Thanksgiving is just a few weeks away, and I don't think he has anyone to spend it with. Doesn't that bother you?"

At that, Skye asked, "Well, don't you, your parents, or even someone else in the neighborhood know anything more about him? Your family has lived here since you were born."

Embarrassed, I replied, "I've asked my mom a couple of times about him, but both times she replied she didn't know anything other than the rumors going around, and that it wasn't any of my business. She told me to forget about it and reminded me to never go near the manor."

Addy inquired, "What about your dad? Did you ask him too?"

I replied, "Well, yes, but my dad won't usually answer questions when he doesn't want to, so he never told me anything."

At that time, we had entered the school grounds and went off to our classes. After a long and tiring day, we gathered together to walk home.

Addy asked, "Well, did either of your reading buddies give you a nasty time?"

I tried not to chuckle as I replied, "No, luckily mine was out sick."

Addy looked expectantly at Skye, who replied in total disgust, "Mine got sick while I was reading to him and threw up!"

Addy suppressed a giggle and said, "I hope it wasn't because of what you were reading to him."

Skye scowled and replied, "NO! Actually, he had filled his lunch box with leftover Halloween candy and stuffed himself with it during lunch. It was so disgusting, and the smell was even worse!" She continued, "Even now, when I breathe in, I can still smell it."

Addy, appearing shame-faced, said apologetically, "I'm really sorry, Skye. I shouldn't have laughed at that."

Skye replied, "That's all right, Addy. I understand. In a few years, I'll probably look back and laugh about it myself. At least the vomit missed me completely. By the way, how did Jeffrey treat you today?"

Addy said delightedly, "He was out today, and he'll be out tomorrow too! But that's not the best part. At lunch, Marty whispered to me that he had heard Jeffrey say something about him moving away. Wouldn't that be terrific?"

I responded, "Totally awesome!"

Tuesday passed without any surprises. I was glad that I had another interesting book to read. When I got tired of reading, I worked on drawing, painting, or practicing my step dancing. Thank goodness, my parents didn't take away my art supplies, or I would have gone completely insane! I couldn't wait for Wednesday night, as Skye and I had choir practice at our church, and my mother agreed to let me go.

When Wednesday finally arrived, I knew Mr. Balhooner would be more than happy to see us at practice. We always made the night extra fun for him. Once Skye had received permission to join the choir, we asked my mom if we could go a little early each week to help Mr. Balhooner—whom we called Mr. Dude—set everything up. I think she knew from overhearing some of our conversations that we were really going early to "prepare" little pranks on Mr. Balhooner. My mom gave us permission after we explained what we were going to do. I think she actually found it funny to learn what we had planned for the next practice!

Wednesday night choir practice finally arrived. Skye and I were ready to play "church mice" and come up with a plan to trick Mr. Dude while having lots of fun before practice began. We started by hiding in the kitchen. Mr. Balhooner always came in, turned on the light, and poured himself a cup of coffee or a glass of apple cider. We left a note on the fridge door that stated, "No cider on Wednesday night!" On the coffee maker, we attached a sign reading, "Broken, come back next week!"

He came in as usual, and after reading the notes, he groaned and grumbled to himself, "I think there are some mischievous church mice at work here." With that, he turned and headed back toward the kitchen door to leave.

Lickity split; I sprang from my hiding place and aimed a sure-shot hair band at the back of his head, then dove back into hiding. It was an exact hit! POW!

He snapped around, immediately spotted the hair band lying on the kitchen floor, and grabbed it. Whistling, he said in a casual voice, "Well, well, one of my little church mice has apparently lost a hair band. Thank you very much, as I needed one desperately! In fact, next week when I'm here, try to bring another one because I really need two! I've always wanted pigtails!"

We waited a few minutes after he had left the kitchen before Skye and I crept out from our hiding places and burst into laughter! Skye gasped, "He doesn't need hair bands! He's bald!"

I giggled back, "Well, he's not exactly bald, but he definitely doesn't need my hair bands! How am I going to talk to him into giving it back?"

Skye replied, "We'll think of something. Besides, I think he 'wants' us to come up with something."

I asked, "What do you mean?"

Skye said with a sly grin, "I think he's having as much fun as we are!"

I laughed and replied, "You're right! Maybe next week we can plan to take his hat and then exchange it for my hair band."

Skye and I both were giggling as we started walking up to the balcony to begin singing.

The balance of the week flew by. Friday night, while lying in bed, I thought about everything that had happened in my life since my two friends had arrived. I was so grateful for them and the adventures we had already shared. It was at that moment that I realized something special. My life felt complete. Until then, I guess I had always felt something was wrong or missing. In the past, I thought it was because I never knew my brother, but now I knew it was more than that. Until now, I never had someone who I could confide in and share adventures with. Suddenly, I was so thankful. Then my thoughts shifted to Thanksgiving, which was less than two weeks away, and I immediately started to think of old Mr. Grimly again.

No one ever goes over to the manor, I thought to myself. *How horrible it must be on Thanksgiving not to be able to share it with someone.*

It really bothered me that someone would be alone on a holiday meant for thankfulness. All at once, I came up with the idea that maybe we could invite Mr. Grimly to our house for Thanksgiving!

After thinking the idea over for a short time, I finally decided to ask my parents the next day.

After breakfast the following morning, I got up the courage and asked my parents about inviting him to dinner.

My mom said, "If it really means that much to you, Leira, I'll go over and see if he will answer the door. But I have to tell you that since we've lived here, he has never ventured out of the house. I've heard quite a bit about him from some of the other people in the neighborhood, but that doesn't necessarily mean it's the truth. We'll discuss it sometime. By the way, we're having a large family gathering here for Thanksgiving, so please understand it's not the first thing on my mind. But if you think of any other good ideas to get Mr. Grimly out of his shell, then let's talk about it some more. I honestly believe that he needs a friend too."

Then I prodded Dad for his answer. He responded after a few moments with "Hmm, we'll see." That was the end of the conversation, but knowing Dad, that was an interesting and hopeful reply.

Chapter 16
Thanksgiving

THE NEXT DAY after school, as Thanksgiving was quickly approaching, I asked Addy and Skye once more what they thought about inviting Mr. Grimly to dinner. Addy answered thoughtfully, "I think that it's a terrific idea. My mom and dad are home, so I'll go ask them now."

Skye added, "I'll wait to hear what your parents say before I ask mine. I don't think he needs three dinners!"

Addy returned pretty quickly. She said sorrowfully, "They told me they didn't know anything about him and that they were too busy getting the house ready for our relatives that are coming. I'm sorry. I hope one of your families will say yes."

I tried to cheer up Addy by saying, "Don't worry yet. My mom said she's going over to see if Mr. Grimly will speak with her. It's still possible our family will invite him over."

Skye said with determination, "I won't wait for that! I'm going to ask my parents right now. Hopefully, I'll be back shortly with a big thumbs-up! Keep your fingers crossed!"

After Skye left, Addy and I agreed we'd be more than a little surprised if her parents said yes. Even though Skye was acting confident, neither of us felt as optimistic. While we both waited anxiously for her to return, I glanced down the street to Mrs. Crimpton's home, which was next to Addy's. Startled, I blurted out, "Addy, look at Mrs. Crimpton's house! There's a For Sale sign posted in the front yard! They must have just put that up today. Do you know anything about it?"

Addy replied, "No, it's the first time I've seen it. Wow, wouldn't it be terrific to get rid of that old busybody? Maybe I'll get some really nice new neighbors!"

I replied, "Yeah, but we'll miss all the great gossip in the neighborhood."

Addy looked at me skeptically and stated, "I think the three of us are more than capable of figuring out what's happening. Don't you?"

I was about to reply when I saw Skye walking back across the street. It was obvious from her expression that her parents had also said no. When she reached us, she said, "I didn't have any luck either. My mom is so exhausted from moving in, throwing me a birthday party, and getting ready for Thanksgiving that I didn't even try and ask my dad. My mom told me that Aunt Lizzie and Uncle George are coming with their 'darling' son George Jr. She's my dad's sister, and she and Uncle Frank are really rich and complete snobs. I hate seeing them. They're flying here from Texas. I think the only reason they're coming is to try and find something wrong with our new home."

Addy scrunched up her face and said sympathetically, "They sound horrible. No wonder why your mother is freaked out." Addy then turned to me and said, "Well, Leira, you're our only hope now for Mr. Grimly. When was your mother going to speak to him?"

I replied, "Today, when she gets home from work. While we're waiting, let's go find a game to play. She should be home anytime now." After hurrying into my house, we headed toward the family room, where my mom kept all our games stuffed in a cabinet. It took us awhile to agree on what to play, but we finally chose a trivia video game about movies. Just as we were about to start playing, I noticed my mom passing by. I jumped up and ran out calling, "Mom! How long have you been home? Are you going to Grimly Manor now? Can we come with you?"

My mom raised her hands and said, "Hang on a minute! I only worked a half day today because I have a business trip tomorrow. So I've already been to Grimly Manor."

Addy and Skye, overhearing the conversation, raced to my side as I jumped up and down and urgently asked, "Well, did he answer the door? Did you talk to him? Is he coming for Thanksgiving?"

Mom looked at me sadly and replied, "I'm sorry, Leira, but he wouldn't answer the door, even though I waited for ten minutes and knocked several times."

Instantly, there was total silence as all three of us felt defeated. Mom tried to make us feel better by saying, "Don't worry, there will be other opportunities. Dad and I will make another effort to speak to him."

At that point, none of us felt like playing a game or even being together, so Skye and Addy returned home to work on school projects.

As the week progressed, we discussed what else we might be able to do for Mr. Grimly. Finally, we came up with a terrific plan. As all of us were having our Thanksgiving dinner during midafternoon, we each decided to gather some of the food we were having and hide it away. I had a beautiful basket that I had received one Easter that we could use to carry everything in. Addy and Skye agreed they could each scrounge up a few plastic containers to put their food in.

I asked, "Are you sure they won't be missed?"

Addy replied, "My mom always has a stockpile of disposable containers, so I don't think she'll miss a few."

As I was looking expectantly at Skye for a reply, she laughed and said, "My mom is sooo disorganized right now, I'm not sure if she'd even miss me!"

We talked about what we were having for Thanksgiving and decided on who would bring which foods. I said, "I'll get some turkey, rutabagas, and green bean casserole."

Skye added, "I'll get stuffing, gravy, and butternut squash."

Then Addy said, "I'll bring the mashed potatoes, cranberry sauce, and a piece of pumpkin pie!" We all agreed that it would be a perfect Thanksgiving feast for Mr. Grimly!

On Thanksgiving Day, we were ready to make our plan happen. After all, Mr. Grimly deserved a Thanksgiving dinner as much as, or even more than, we did. At least we had family and friends to share it with.

We decided not to let our parents know about what we were going to do. We didn't want even one of them to say no.

It was a little more difficult than I imagined taking the portions of food. When my mom asked what I was doing with another huge helping, I replied, "Well, Mom, I'm still hungry, and there's a really good show on TV, so I thought I would just go up to my room and nibble on it." Turning around and breathing a sigh of relief, I hurried to my room with a plate full of turkey, rutabagas, and casserole, then stowed them away in a few containers I had gotten earlier.

My bathroom had an awesome heated towel rack, and I covered my basket with several towels to keep it warm and fresh. We had previously decided to get together at seven o'clock. With my basket ready, I looked out the window and wondered if Addy and Skye had succeeded also. It was six thirty, so I only had thirty minutes to wait.

Skye, in the meantime, had a house overflowing with friends and slightly "nasty" relatives. She quickly gathered up extra helpings of stuffing, gravy, and squash and headed straight to her room! She switched her light on and started packing everything in containers. The signal we had arranged was simple. When everything was ready, we were to turn our bedroom lights on. After I saw Skye's light up, I waited for Addy to signal Skye because her dinner had started a little later than ours.

As I couldn't see Addy's bedroom, Skye was to turn her lights on and off a couple of times when Addy's light went on. That was the final signal we were waiting for, so I waited as patiently as I could for the go-ahead.

Finally, at six forty-five, I knew Addy was ready because Skye began flicking her lights. According to the plan, we met at seven o'clock at the old sycamore tree to the left of Addy's house and combined all our goodies into my large basket with a note. Accompanying us were Lucky and Addy's dog Shaggy. That had also been part of the plan, which Addy had brilliantly come up with—of course. We needed to make sure we'd have a reason to leave the house for a while.

The note read,

Dear Mr. Grimly,

We're sorry that you (and Puffin) cannot share Thanksgiving with us, but we hope that this big basket *of terrific food will find a yummy home in both of your tummies! Happy Thanksgiving and best wishes to both of you!*

*Sincerely,
Addy Davies, Skye Finnegan,
and Leira MacGregor*

We quietly made our way up to his door and set the basket down. Then we gave the door three huge raps. We instantly heard Puffin barking inside, and both Lucky and Shaggy responded by barking back. Without waiting for an answer, we turned around and started walking back toward our homes, tugging constantly on Lucky's and Shaggy's leashes.

Each of us hoped he would take our basket of goodies and enjoy it. We stopped at Skye's house to give the dogs a bit more playtime—and us more time to keep an eye on the front door of Grimly Manor. We sat on Skye's front porch and watched the manor for about twenty minutes. When the twenty minutes were up, Addy and I told Skye it was time for us to go home. We were disappointed not to see Mr. Grimly, but at the same time, it felt good that we had accomplished what we set out to do.

The next day, the basket was gone, so we assumed Mr. Grimly (and Puffin) had enjoyed its contents. Over the next few weeks, we talked about how we should have stayed up in shifts that night and kept watch on the manor. After discussing it for about the tenth time, I said, "It wouldn't have worked anyway."

Skye asked, "Why not?"

I replied, "Well, we all had a ton of turkey to eat, and you know what they say."

Addy looked perplexed and said, "No, what?"

I replied, "My mom says there are enzymes or whatever in turkey that makes you sleepy, so we never would have been able to stay awake even if we had tried."

"Oh," replied Addy. "Leira, by the way, did you ask your mom if she knew anything about Mrs. Crimpton's house being put up for sale?"

I felt like an idiot as I replied, "Duh! I forgot to tell you, I asked my mom last week, and she said Mrs. Crimpton was going to Alabama to live with her daughter. She decided she didn't need such a large house anymore, plus she's having trouble remembering things! I don't envy her new neighbors. Can you imagine a gossipy old lady with a bad memory?" All of us tried to suppress our giggles.

Then, Skye sarcastically asked, "Well, who's the one who forgot to tell us about it?"

Addy started laughing hysterically as I replied, "OK, OK, the laughs are on me!"

Chapter 17
Caroling

THERE WERE ONLY three and a half weeks until Christmas, and as always, we decorated the house the first weekend of December. It was hard work but fun too. My mom did most of it while playing Scottish Christmas tunes. First, she put up the decorations around the house. The Christmas village she had made by hand usually went up first, as there was a lot of work to setting it up. Throughout the village, my mom placed tiny old-fashioned lampposts that actually lit up. I helped place the cottony "snow" around and on the pieces after she finished arranging everything. Every year, Mom made a new piece to add. This year she made "the Train Station." We always placed the newest addition on top of our antique stereo positioned in the middle of the village.

Mom had gathered so many beautiful Christmas decorations over the years. Some of them were very special. My Grandma Armstrong (my mom's mother) had given each of her three children beautiful bell angels, which had been handed down to her by my great-grandmother. Mom always told me so many incredible stories from her childhood while we were decorating.

Once she had put the tree together, I helped her string on the lights and garland, then carefully hung the ornaments. When everything was complete, we lit up the mistletoe-scented candle. If you closed your eyes and breathed deeply, you could imagine yourself standing in the middle of a fragrant pine forest. It was even more beautiful at night with the Christmas village glowing in the background and the ornaments shining off the colored lights on the tree.

After the tree was finished, we arranged all our presents beneath it, including my gifts to Addy and Skye. I had gotten each of them a large Beanie Buddy with a necklace hanging on it, along with earrings and a bracelet. I really hoped that they would like them!

On Tuesday, the weather was a little warmer, which felt so nice after too many days of freezing cold. So I asked my mom if I could walk home from school with Addy and Skye. As the morning was still pretty cold, Mom was driving us to school.

My mother replied, "I don't see why not. It's going to be a beautiful day, and I'm sure there won't be many more like it." She called Skye's and Addy's parents, who gave their permission.

On our way home from school, I asked my friends, "Even though Mr. Grimly didn't say anything about our Thanksgiving basket, don't you think we should do something again for Christmas?"

Skye responded, "Like what? Do you have an idea?"

With a sigh, I replied, "Not really. Can either of you think of something?"

We were all silent for a while. Then Addy exclaimed, "I've got a terrific idea! Let's go caroling! He's sure to hear us and come to the door. Maybe we could leave him and Puffin a nice gift also. What do you think?" Skye and I agreed wholeheartedly.

Then I asked Addy, "Have you heard any more about Jeffrey moving?"

Addy replied, "Yes! I'm glad you brought that up. He's definitely moving and soon, either this month or next. Isn't that fantastic? He's been totally rotten to me since I refused to go out with him. He's constantly trying to take my mind off my work or get me in trouble. Thankfully, Ms. Oldman sees right through him. I think she'll be happy when he moves to a different school too."

Skye asked, "Do you know where he's going to? Is it a different state or just another town?"

Addy replied, "No, I don't know. It's really weird. He's keeping very quiet about that. I can't imagine why he wouldn't want to tell anyone, unless it's embarrassing or something. Maybe we'll never know. But either way, I don't care where he goes as long as it's far away from here!"

The next few weeks passed quickly. With only four days left until Christmas, our final day of school arrived before vacation. Unfortunately, a slight problem arose. We had planned to go caroling that night, but as I looked out my classroom window, I noticed it was snowing. Within an hour, an announcement came across the loudspeaker that we were having early dismissal. The whole class shouted, "Hurray!"

Mom picked us up and said, "You're not going to believe this, but we're supposed to get at least eight inches of snow! It's not supposed to stop until sometime after midnight."

Concerned, I asked my mom, "Can we still go caroling tonight?"

She replied, "I'll see what it looks like by nightfall, and as long as Skye's and Addy's parents say it's all right, I don't see why not. But I won't make any promises until then." We watched with growing excitement as it started to snow more heavily.

After my mother pulled into our driveway, both Skye and Addy came in with us because their parents weren't home yet. Both of them called their mothers at work and received permission to go caroling as long as the weather wasn't too bad.

Then we hurried up to my bedroom and started practicing the three carols we would be singing. We had each chosen our favorite ones. I asked, "Is it all right if we sing 'Do You Hear What I Hear' first?"

Skye shrugged her shoulders and said, "I guess."

Addy didn't seem to mind and said, "OK, now let's practice."

As Addy and I started singing, Skye interrupted and said, "But let's do 'Joy to the World' after that. Then, we can finish with Addy's favorite, 'Silent Night.'"

I looked at Addy for approval, and she replied tactfully, "That's good because we're going to sing only one song per house, and there are eighteen houses on the street, so we'll each get to sing our favorite song six times."

I started to count up the houses and realized that Mr. Grimly's manor would be number six. I asked Addy and Skye, "Do you know which song we'll be singing at Grimly Manor?"

Skye asked thoughtfully, "Whose house are we starting with?"

I replied, "My house, then Addy's." I could see them both working it out, and when Addy finally figured it out, she broke out into a huge grin!

Addy replied gleefully, "'Silent Night'!"

As the afternoon wore on, both of my friends went home to get their snowsuits. There was already about three inches of snow on the ground, and we still had about an hour before it got dark. I had a small hill down my backyard, so the three of us went sledding.

After a while, my mom yelled for us to come in. She had steaming hot chocolate and fresh baked corn muffins waiting for us. The smell was so incredible. We took off our snowsuits faster than ever, and within moments, we were eating our muffins and sipping our "really hot" hot chocolate.

Mom reentered the room and said, "I've just gotten off the phone with Mrs. Finnegan and Mr. Davies. I wanted to go over the current weather situation with them. They both agreed you could do some caroling. But instead of eighteen houses, we only want you to do twelve because it's snowing very heavily. I've brought out the electric candles to light your way. Now finish up your treats and get going. Dad and I will be waiting for you to ring our doorbell first!"

The snow was now about five inches deep as we started singing at my house. Then we slowly worked our way toward Grimly Manor.

After caroling at Addy's house, Skye said, "I brought a humongous steak bone to leave for Puffin. What did you guys bring?"

Addy replied, "I made a Christmas card with a picture I drew of him and Puffin by the Christmas tree, and the three of us singing outside."

I said, "Wow, Addy! That sounds terrific! You should have shown it to us before we left. I'm giving him a special handmade ornament to go on his tree and a dog biscuit for Puffin. I think that all our gifts will cheer him up. Come on, let's keep going."

The next stop was Mrs. Crimpton's house. She was absolutely delighted to hear us sing. She pleaded, "Can't you please sing another song? You all sound so lovely."

I replied, "I'm sorry, Mrs. Crimpton, but we only have a short time to go caroling because of the storm. But maybe you'll be able to hear us when we sing at the next house." Mrs. Crimpton understood and, smiling, thanked us for coming.

We caroled at two more homes prior to reaching Grimly Manor. We stared in awe at the beautifully lit decorations. We plowed our way through the snow and knocked loudly on the door. Immediately Puffin started barking like crazy. We waited a minute, knocked again, and then started singing "Silent Night." When we were about halfway through, we noticed the door open a few inches, but the only thing we could see was Puffin. She was sitting with her tongue hanging out, and her tail was wagging happily.

After we finished singing, Addy said cheerfully, "Hello, Puffin. Hello, Mr. Grimly. We've brought you a few gifts. We'll just leave them here on the porch. They're for you and Puffin. Don't leave them too long, or they'll get covered in snow!"

Together, we called out, "Merry Christmas!" As we turned around and began plowing back through the snow, we thought we heard a voice say, "Merry Christmas to you too, my little angels."

By then we were so exhausted we decided we'd had enough caroling for one night, so we all agreed to head home. On the way, I asked Skye and Addy, "Did either of you hear those strange noises coming from inside the manor?"

Skye replied, "I did. It was really creepy because it sounded like something between a squeak and a squeal. I have no idea what would make that sound."

Addy commented, "Well, I didn't hear a thing, but I did notice that Puffin seemed a bit skinnier. Maybe Mr. Grimly has put her on a diet! But I think both of you were imagining those sounds!"

Skye retorted, "And I believe someone needs to get their hearing checked!"

"All right, you guys, that's enough!" I said, "Let's just get home and chill out." That phrase made both Skye and Addy laugh before I even knew why.

After realizing I had used the word *chill*, I chuckled too, then continued, "We've done enough for tonight." Addy and Skye nodded. As we finished our walk home, we wondered if Mr. Grimly would like our gifts and agreed we should tell our parents about them, as well as the Thanksgiving treats we had left him.

While lying awake in bed that night, I wondered if we'd really get eight inches of snow. The weatherman seemed to mess up a lot.

When I awoke the next morning, I was in for the shock of my life!

Chapter 18
Snowed In

I JUMPED OUT of bed early the next morning. Christmas Eve day was tomorrow, and I was getting so excited! After glancing out the window on the way to my closet, I stopped dead in my tracks. Walking slowly back toward the window, I blinked several times to make sure I wasn't imagining what I had seen. After placing my hands on the windowsill and pressing my nose against the glass, I thought to myself, *That's not eight inches of snow. That's not even a foot of snow. That's at least* two feet *of snow!* With my heart pounding, I grabbed my robe, stuffed my feet into some fluffy slippers, and raced downstairs as fast as possible. When I hit the last step, I hung onto the banister and swung myself around toward the dining room, running straight into my dad!

Dad stated simply, "It's too early in the morning to be tackled."

I gasped, "Dad, have you looked outside? There's a mountain of snow out there. Where are Mom, Lucky, and Emmy? Is everyone all right? I don't know whether to be excited or frightened! Do you think we'll lose power? Are the phones working?" Desperately, I pleaded, "Dad, why aren't you answering me?"

Dad replied in his usual calm voice, "Umm… well, let me think." He rubbed his chin thoughtfully as I was about ready to scream! Finally, after what seemed like forever, he said, "There's definitely a lot of snow out there."

After he didn't continue fast enough for me, I jumped up and down and asked a bit sarcastically, "And why is there soooo much snow?"

Dad replied, "Well, apparently, the weather guys got it wrong because we ended up getting hit by a nor'easter, which—I guess—they were clueless about until it happened."

Frustrated, I asked, "What the heck is a nor'easter'?"

Dad continued, "Basically, it means that the storm kept turning back around toward us."

Impatiently I asked, "Where's Mom?"

Dad replied, "She's in the kitchen."

As I raced into the kitchen, my senses were immediately filled with the delicious smell of bacon—my favorite! After clearing my head for a second, I quickly asked Mom, "What's going on? I asked Dad about a bunch of things, but he wouldn't answer all my questions. By the way—what are you making besides bacon?"

My mom smiled and said we were having eggs, bacon, and hash browns, because we're going to need the energy to dig ourselves out.

As I was trying to figure out what that meant, Dad entered and said, "Lucky and Emmy are fine, although they need to go outside. We didn't lose power—as you might have noticed—and you can call whoever you want—but not right now."

My mother continued the conversation by saying, "Your father stayed up until one o'clock in the morning shoveling an area outside for Lucky and Emmy to make sure they could get out to do their business. When he finally got to bed, there was a little over a foot of snow. He thought it was tapering off, but obviously, it didn't. Let's have breakfast, and Dad and I will explain what we need to do."

The aroma was so delicious that my stomach gave out an enormous grumble. I grabbed a plate and said, "Mom, can you fill it up please?" I couldn't believe that she gave me extra bacon—she didn't usually do that. I grabbed a seat at our kitchen table and quickly ate everything on my plate. I finished before my parents were done and asked, "All right, you said you'd tell me what 'we' need to do. So what do I have to do?"

Mom and Dad gave each other a curious look, and then Mom said, "First, I want you to get dressed and put your snowsuit on. I'll have everything set out by the time you come back downstairs."

With delight twinkling in my eyes, I responded happily, "Does that mean I get to go sledding right away? Can I call Skye and Addy?"

My mother interrupted, "There's something important we need to have done first, and you're the only one who can do it."

Hesitantly I asked, "And—what do I have to do?"

Mom inhaled deeply and replied, "Despite all the shoveling Daddy did last night, we still can't open the outside door. The snow got heavier after Daddy went to bed, and now there's more than two feet of snow out there. Since you can still squiggle through the doggie door, we need you to…"

I blurted out, "You actually want *me* to go through the doggie door, underneath the snow? There's positively *no way* I'm tunneling through the snow!"

Mom insisted that I wouldn't have any problem. "Daddy will hold your feet and as soon as you're through the door, you'll be able to poke your arms up through the snow. At that point, you'll just need to wiggle up about six inches and stand up. The snow's extremely light and fluffy."

She noticed by my expression that I wasn't convinced, so she continued to try and change my mind (like all parents do) by adding, "Of course, if you're totally against the idea, then Dad could always remove a window and jump down, but this way would be much more simple and quicker. What do you think?"

Smartly, after hesitating for a moment, I replied, "Sorry, Mom, but I don't want to do it. It's too scary. But you or Daddy can jump out through the window, and I'll be more than happy to watch."

Mom replied, "Oh, and I thought you wanted me to enter us in the mother-daughter *Fear Factor* show. I guess that went 'right out the window'!"

I was completely embarrassed and angry that she said that. Before I could respond, Dad said calmly, "Well, I guess the twenty dollars is mine." He turned and began walking toward the coat closet.

I exclaimed, "What twenty dollars?"

My mom responded, "I offered Dad twenty dollars to jump out the window, but he suggested that I offer it to you first."

I quickly rethought everything, and then I turned to Dad and said with a gulp, "I'm ready to play *Fear Factor* and go through the door—as long as there's twenty bucks waiting for me!"

Mom responded, "Not in your pajamas, you're not! And if Dad has to pull you back in and jump through the window, the money is his."

With a nod, I replied, "OK! But the cash is definitely mine!" I rushed upstairs to get dressed while my mom put my snow stuff together.

When I was finished bundling up, my dad instructed, "After you're able to stand up, there should be less than a foot and a half of snow from here to the back door. Just make your way through it, and clear the area surrounding the door enough so we can open it. I left the shovel next to the porch. Are you ready?"

I replied with determination, "Absolutely, but you'd better have that twenty dollars waiting for me at the door!" Eventually after calming myself, I took a deep breath and thought, *This is exactly like being on an episode of children's* Fear Factor. I couldn't wait to tell Skye and Addy. With my dad behind me, I crawled through the doggie door as quickly as possible. It was seriously scary—for about five seconds—then I popped my arms up through the snow, sprang up, and, with a victorious smile on my face, yelled, "I DID IT!" I proceeded to tread through the powdery snow. Arriving at the back door, I quickly cleaned it off with the shovel my dad had left. Mom and Dad were anxiously waiting for me when I swung the door open and exclaimed, "Ta-da! Where's my twenty bucks?"

Dad grinned slightly and handed me the money while Mom scooped up my snowy things and handed me a huge cup of steaming hot chocolate.

I grabbed the portable phone and walked into the living room, carefully holding the hot mug in my other hand. Then sinking down into my favorite comfy chair, I called Addy's house. Her mother answered and promptly replied, "Here she is, but could you please keep the conversation brief, because we have other people to call."

I replied, "No problem, Mrs. Davies, thanks!" When Addy picked up the phone, I said, "Have I got an interesting story for you.

Unfortunately, your mom says we can't talk long so I'll just have to give you the shortened version."

When I finished, she replied, "That's insane! I can't believe you actually did it! It's too bad we don't have a doggie door! I sure would have liked to make some money too! Anyway, my dad has almost finished taking out the windows and screen, and he's dressed to jump! Maybe I should ask them to pay me to jump? I'll have to talk to you later and let you know what happens. Why don't you call Skye? I have to go."

I quickly responded, "All right, I'll phone Skye now and meet you later. Maybe we can go sledding together! Tell your dad I said, 'Good luck and that if you'd just waited a little while longer, I could have come over and dug you out!' Hopefully, I'll see you soon."

With that, I hung up and dialed Skye's number. The answering machine picked up, so I glanced out the window toward Skye's house. Her entire family was already outside, plowing, shoveling, and playing. I hurried into the kitchen and asked my mom if I could go join them.

She replied, "All right, but just for a little while. There's plenty of shoveling that you should help with right here."

I responded, "OK, no problem. I'll only stay about a half hour. Then I'll come back here and help you and Dad. I love you!"

She beamed at me, gave me a huge hug, and said, "I love you too, and I'm proud of you for being so brave." Then with a twinkle of understanding reflected in her eyes, she said, "By the way, I know you didn't do it for the money. You did it for us, and I thank you with all my heart."

My eyes shifted away in embarrassment because she always had me figured out. I lifted my chin up and replied, "Mom, really, I just didn't want Dad to get the money, so there!" We both started laughing.

Mom said with tears of happiness in her eyes, "I won't tell Dad if you don't."

I replied, "Not a chance! Well, maybe…" I left as quickly as possible to go over Skye's house. On the way there, I glanced down the street toward Grimly Manor and wondered who was going to plow Mr. Grimly's driveway. Then I noticed a strange thing: the For Sale sign in front of Mrs. Crimpton's house was gone. I thought to myself, It probably just fell over during the storm.

Chapter 19
Christmas Surprise!

THE FOLLOWING MORNING, on Christmas Eve day, I received an unusual-looking letter in the mail. There was no return address, so I opened it cautiously.

It said,

Dear Leira,

I want to thank you and your friends personally for finding my dog, Puffin. If you hadn't returned her to me on Halloween, something horrifying might have happened. Instead, something wonderful occurred that night. I want to share it with all three of you. I understand that you might be a little nervous to come inside and receive your gifts, so I'll leave them outside my front door at two o'clock in the afternoon, tomorrow on Christmas Day. If you don't come by three o'clock, I'll understand and take the presents back inside. Please know that these are gifts from my heart.

Sincerely,

Mr. Grimly

I immediately called Skye's house, and luckily, she answered the phone. Excitedly, I asked her, "Did you get your mail today?"

Skye replied, "I don't think so. Why? What's going on?"

I exclaimed, "Just run out and get your mail and see if there's a letter for you! Hurry up!"

Skye declared, "All right, I'm going." When she returned moments later, she said curiously, "Yeah, I received a letter. Who's it from?"

I urgently replied, "Just open it!"

Skye burst out, "Oh my goodness! It's from Mr. Grimly, and it says he's leaving presents for us tomorrow. Did you get a letter like mine?"

I responded, "Of course I did! That's why I called. Ask your mom if you can run over to Addy's house with me for a little while."

She replied, "Hang on a minute." When Skye returned to the phone, she said, "My mom said no problem, so I'll meet you outside in about three minutes."

While putting on my winter coat and snow boots, I shouted, "Hey, Mom! Can I go over Addy's house for a little while with Skye? It's really important."

Mom answered, "OK, but just for thirty minutes, because lunch will be ready soon." She added, "Oh! I forgot to tell you, we found out a little more about the neighbors moving in next to Addy. I'm not exactly sure how to pronounce their last name, but it's spelled K-U-V-A-S-C."

My eyes widened in horror as I fearfully asked, "They wouldn't possibly have a son named Jeffrey, would they?"

My mother peered around the corner at me and asked with concern, "Yes, I think they do. Why? Do you know him?"

With a grimace, I replied, "I do—unfortunately. That's the worst news I've heard all year."

Mom gently asked me, "Do you want to talk to me about him?"

I replied, "Later. Right now, I need to go meet Skye and Addy."

My mom nodded her head and said, "Go on then."

Skye was halfway to Addy's front door by the time I shook off the shock and left the house. I caught up with her, and we knocked on the door together. Her little sister, Josie, politely answered the door, and then at the sight of us, her expression turned into a scowl, and she started yelling back over her shoulder, "Addy, your stupid friends are here!"

As Addy came toward the door, she angrily said to Josie, "Don't ever use those words or that nasty voice when you're talking about my friends! Go back to the table right now. I'll be there in a few minutes."

Glancing back at us, Addy said, "I'm so sorry about her. Unfortunately I can't come out right now because Mom says I have to finish the puzzle that Josie and I are working on first." I noticed Josie's smug smile as she lingered in the background.

I hurriedly replied, "We're not here to play. We've come to find out if you received a letter in the mail today."

Addy answered, "I'm not sure. Mom or Dad always picks up the mail. Why, is everything all right? What's happened?"

Josie interrupted, "Yeah, what's going on?" Then she unexpectedly raced off calling, "Mom, Dad! Did Addy get a secret letter today?" Addy flew off after her.

She hurried back a few minutes later, letter in hand with Josie right behind her. Addy sternly said, "Get back to that puzzle right now! I said I'd only be a couple of minutes. If you don't leave this instant, I won't help you anymore!"

Josie smugly replied back, "Mom said you have to!"

Mrs. Davies appeared from around the corner and told Josie she needed to return to the puzzle immediately. Then she turned to Addy and firmly said, "You have five minutes to spend with your friends." Then she turned to us and said, "Hello, ladies, please come in and warm yourselves up for a few minutes."

Skye and I sat down in the living room with our letters while Addy carefully opened hers and read it. She looked up in astonishment when she finished. Both Skye and I held ours up so Addy could understand that we had received similar letters.

I inquisitively asked Skye and Addy, "Well? What do you think we should do?"

Addy stated simply, "Isn't it obvious? We should go there at two o'clock tomorrow afternoon."

Skye hesitated but finally declared, "I agree."

I thought about it for a moment and said, "Awesome! But don't you think we should tell our parents about it first?" Addy and Skye nodded in agreement.

Just before leaving, I remembered what my mom had told me, and I stated grimly, "I have another piece of information that neither of you will like, to put it mildly."

Skye asked with trepidation, "What is it?"

I glanced from Skye to Addy, licked my dry lips, and stated nervously, "I know where Jeffrey is moving to."

Addy urged, "Well, don't leave us in suspense. Where is he moving to and why wouldn't we like the answer?"

I took a deep breath and said, "He's moving in to old Mrs. Crimpton's house right next door to you, Addy."

Addy exclaimed in disbelief, "That's impossible! It can't be true! Are you absolutely positive?"

Nodding my head, I replied, "Yes, I'm really sorry. My mother told me just before I left to come over here." Addy covered her face with her hands, while Skye and I watched sympathetically. We both sat down on either side of her and gave her a huge hug.

Then Skye commented, "Don't be too upset, you've got both of us, remember?"

Addy looked up at us teary-eyed and replied, "I'm counting on that."

On our way out the door, I said, "Cheer up, don't forget about tomorrow! I can't wait to see what Mr. Grimly got for us, but at the same time—I think I'll be a little nervous too. Anyway, tonight's Christmas Eve! Don't spoil it by worrying about that idiot. At least until after the holidays." Giving her a final hug before we headed back home, I could see Josie near the table, pretending to be searching for a piece of the puzzle. But I knew the only puzzle she wanted to figure out was the one about her sister, the letter, and why Addy was crying.

Our family enjoyed a peaceful Christmas Eve and filled ourselves with yummy-tasting appetizers of crackers, cheese, fudge, and fruit. My mom even made my grandma Armstrong's favorite recipe of penuche, which is a type of maple fudge. We sang Christmas carols and silently gazed at our beautiful tree with its sparkling tiny lights, and the fragrance of the mistletoe Christmas candle scented the whole room. It was a memory I would cherish forever.

The next thing I knew it was Christmas morning! Although I was thrilled about all the wonderful presents I had opened, I couldn't help but wonder in the back of my mind about Mr. Grimly and his letter. While my mother started preparing Christmas dinner, I had plenty of time to check out each gift. Dad helped me set up some games. Unfortunately, there was nothing I could do to stop myself from looking at my watch every few minutes. Skye, Addy, and I really hadn't had any time to talk about what would happen this afternoon. We each received permission to go pick up the presents at Grimly Manor. We had already told our parents about what we had been doing for Mr. Grimly. My mother had been shocked that the three of us had found the courage to approach Mr. Grimly while nobody else in the neighborhood would. She was also proud of us for being so thoughtful. On the other hand, she lectured me about not telling her or Dad sooner. She made it very clear that we were not to do anything like that again without getting permission first. So I was happily surprised when they agreed to let me go over and pick up my present, as long as Addy and Skye were with me. But knowing my parents, I figured one of them would keep an eye on us.

I phoned Addy immediately after we finished our Christmas dinner. When she answered, I asked, "What do you think? It's almost two o'clock. Should we go now?"

She declared, "Let's do it… but only if Skye is ready to come too."

I replied, "Of course. I'll call her right now and let you know." I dialed Skye's number, and fortunately, she answered. After asking if she was ready to go to Mr. Grimly's, she replied, "I'll be right over!"

I phoned Addy back and told her Skye was ready. We met together in front of Addy's house and walked cautiously toward Grimly Manor. As we started up the driveway, we noticed a large box on the front porch. It wasn't wrapped, but it was topped with a huge red and green bow.

We approached the package with excitement and apprehension. There was a large sign on the outside of the box that read, "Merry Christmas to my three special friends! Please open me up soon so I can say 'Hello.'" We looked at one another with curiosity, wondering whether we should open it or run! Just then, we heard the tiniest yip from inside the box! We looked at each other, took another step forward, and then listened more carefully. Leaning forward, I gave the box a tiny nudge, and a few more yips came out!

Addy noticed a small envelope sticking out from the box. She pulled it out and read aloud, "Hi! We are Katie, Shugar, and Fluffums! Our mom is Puffin! We are gifts to you (if you want us) for taking good care of our mom on Halloween night because that's when we were born! If you're unable to bring us home with you, then just leave us here, and Mr. Grimly will care for us like he does for our mom!"

The three of us gleefully opened the box. Inside were the three cutest puppies we had ever seen! I reached in and pulled out one that was beige and brown. Her legs, belly, and top of her head right down to her little wet nose were beige, and the remainder of her was rusty brown. She was so cuddly! When I held her up, she yipped at me and licked my nose! I said, "This one is definitely mine, and because she's so fluffy, she must be Fluffums!"

Skye was sitting just to the left of me. The creamy-colored puppy was jumping up at her, so smiling, she said, "This must be Shugar, and I think she wants me!"

To my right, Addy watched the remaining black and rusty brown pup that just sat there staring up at her while wagging her tail vigorously. Addy stated, "There's no doubt that Katie was meant for me." She picked her up and cuddled her.

Holding the puppies, we knocked on Mr. Grimly's door to express our thanks and happiness. We tried several times, and although Puffin was barking in the background, no one answered. I looked at Skye and Addy and said, "Let's come back another time. We'd better bring these puppies home."

Addy said, "When we come back, shouldn't we bring him something special to show how much we appreciate his 'gifts'?" Skye nodded in agreement, and we started off to our homes.

There was one problem: were our parents going to let us keep the puppies? When that thought occurred to us, I noticed how the three of us slowed down at the same time. We were scared that one or more of our parents would say no. I left Addy and Skye at their driveways. Overcoming my fear, I entered the back door and immediately ran straight into my mom. Fluffums gave a little yip, and before I could say a word, I noticed my dad was standing right behind my mom. I looked at both of them and felt my stomach flip-flop as I asked in a pleading, tearful voice, "Please… can we keep her? Please? We were each given one of Puffin's three puppies. I'll do anything if I can just keep her. Please?"

Mom and Dad looked at one another a bit strangely, and then turning back to me, Dad said, "It's not our decision."

Confused, I asked, "What does that mean?"

Dad whistled to Lucky, and she came running. Dad replied simply, "It's up to Lucky."

It suddenly dawned on me that my parents had been watching us. Apparently, they had already decided that if Lucky was all right with it, then they were too. Taking a deep breath, I bent down to Lucky and said in a sweet voice, "Here, girl, look what I've brought home. It's a new friend for you to play with." At that, Fluffums yipped, and Lucky came over and sniffed her. Fluffums proceeded to give Lucky several little licks and then yipped again. I anxiously waited to see what Lucky would do. At that point, I decided to put Fluffums down. Much to my amazement, she went straight to Lucky and nuzzled against her. As I watched, Lucky sat down with her tail wagging and barked happily! I looked up at my parents with tears streaming down my face and asked, "Does that mean it's a yes?"

Both of my parents nodded while smiling. Then Mom's smile faded as she said, "Remember, you said you'd do anything. I have a very long list, and I don't want to hear any complaints. Understood?"

I nodded happily and replied, "I'm ready whenever you are."

Mom responded, "You can start with housebreaking her and cleaning up her messes. Also, you'll have to pay out of your allowance for a collar, leash, checkup, and license. Is that clear?"

The realization of the responsibility hit me like a ton of bricks. After a moment, I said, "Yes, I understand."

Then I asked, "I just have one tiny favor. Could you watch Fluffums while I go see if Skye and Addy were able to keep their puppies too?"

Shaking her head, my mom replied, "No, take her with you, and make sure she does her 'business' outside."

I said dismally, "Oh… all right. I'll only be gone for a few minutes."

I hurried outside and put Fluffums down. There was so much snow I wasn't worried about her getting away. As I looked up, I saw Skye was already outside waving her arms happily.

Then we both watched as Addy emerged from her house with Katie in her arms. As she lowered Katie to the ground, she let out a whoop, raised both of her arms, and head toward the sky and yelled, "It's a yes!"

It was the happiest Christmas I'd ever had in my entire life! We would have to think of an awesome way to thank Mr. Grimly.

Chapter 20
A Grimly Ending

IT WAS NEARING dusk when we received permission to take Mr. Grimly some Christmas dinner leftovers. Our parents all agreed to watch the puppies. When we began walking toward the manor, Addy said, "I hope he lets us in. But I am a little nervous."

Skye replied, "Anyone who's been as nice as he has can't be that bad."

I suggested, "Well, if we get too nervous, then we can just stand in the doorway." As we walked up his driveway and neared the porch steps, it started to snow again!

"Awesome!" said Skye. "We'll be able to go sledding for a month with all this snow!" We walked up the steps and knocked on the door. We could hear Puffin barking inside. I guess she knew our scent and figured she didn't need to growl.

After a few minutes, we knocked once again, a little more loudly. Puffin was still barking. We started to worry that something might have happened to Mr. Grimly. We looked at each other, and I asked, "What do you think we should do?"

Skye suggested, "Why don't we yell and tell him it's only us and that we just want to thank him?"

Addy and I agreed. On the count of three, we shouted out together, "Mr. Grimly, it's just us, Skye, Addy, and Leira. Could you please open the door because we've brought a delicious Christmas dinner for you?"

"Yeah," added Skye, "and it's getting really cold and snowy, so could we come in for just a few minutes?"

Puffin stopped barking, and the door opened slightly. Mr. Grimly replied in a sorrowful voice, "You're always welcome here, but please don't be afraid when you see me. I'm just wearing a mask. All right?"

We looked at each other surprisingly, wondering why he was wearing a mask on Christmas. Shrugging our shoulders, Addy answered tentatively, "OK."

The door slowly creaked open, and then without any warning, Puffin immediately ran out jumping up on us! Mr. Grimly turned away from the door and called to Puffin while walking over to a large old-fashioned chair. Puffin obediently followed her owner. As we entered the living room of the manor, Mr. Grimly pointed toward a Victorian sofa next to the fireplace and said, "Please, have a seat."

We walked over to the sofa and sat down. When I finally glanced up at him, I was somewhat startled! The mask he was wearing was different from the one he'd worn on Halloween (thank goodness). It reminded me of the ones I'd seen at the store that were made to look like funny old presidents, but the mask didn't seem funny to me. I inhaled deeply trying to calm myself, then stood up, and walked over to Mr. Grimly. I said as cheerfully as I possibly could, "We've brought you a Christmas dinner to try and thank you for giving us the puppies—well, not only for that reason." I added awkwardly. "We hope you will enjoy it as much or more than your Thanksgiving dinner."

Mr. Grimly gratefully accepted the basket and stood up. "I'll just put this in the kitchen to heat up after you leave. I don't want you to stay too long and get lost in the snow."

Addy actually laughed and said, "I don't think that will happen! We dug ourselves out from the blizzard a few days ago."

When he returned to the living room and sat down, Skye blurted out, "Why are you wearing a mask?" Addy and I were mortified, but to be perfectly honest, I wanted to know too.

Mr. Grimly sighed and said, "Well, I guess the three of you deserve the truth, but I would appreciate it if you wouldn't discuss what I tell you with anyone other than your parents without my permission. I just want to live a quiet life. Well, not quite a quiet life, because I would like you to visit occasionally and bring along those pups so I can see how they are getting along."

I replied, "You have our word of honor." I looked at Skye and Addy, who nodded reassuringly.

Mr. Grimly sighed, "I'll try not to make the story too long. When I was a boy, about ten or eleven, I was playing at my friend's house the next street over. My parents were going to pick me up when it was time to leave. I was excited because they were taking me to a museum in a neighboring town."

He added thoughtfully, "I don't recall which town, but that doesn't matter. Anyway, my friend went downstairs to get something, and suddenly I heard a terrible explosion. I opened the bedroom door and saw smoke billowing up the stairs. It was then that my nightmare began."

Mr. Grimly hung his head low, shaking it, and placed a hand over the mask. We sat silently, waiting for him to regain his composure and continue.

After several moments, he resumed, "At that point I panicked. I quickly ran back into the bedroom and raced to the window. I looked frantically out from the second floor and, with a sigh of relief, saw my parents hurrying toward the house. I threw the window open and screamed, "Mother! Father! There's been an explosion! I can't get down, and Walter might be trapped on the first floor!" Anxiously, I waited for my parents to help Walter and myself.

"I heard my father yelling to my mother to run next door and phone the fire department. Then he hurriedly entered the house. A few minutes later, I saw my mother reappear. I watched my father stumbling from the house, coughing terribly, but with Walter in his arms. I didn't know if my friend was dead or alive. My mother ran over to help Walter while my father proceeded to run back toward the house. I screamed, "MOTHER, DO NOT LET FATHER GO BACK INTO THE HOUSE! THE STAIRCASE IS ON FIRE!" To my horror, my mother started running directly for the front door."

Skye, Addy, and I had tears streaming down our faces as Mr. Grimly continued.

"I was overwhelmed with fear, but I covered my nose and mouth with a handkerchief and ran out the bedroom door to the top of the stairs. Through the smoke, I screamed to my father to get out. When he was more than halfway up the stairs, it suddenly seemed, while trying to see through the dense smoke and flames, that he'd leapt straight up to me! I was much disoriented and barely conscious as I felt him grab hold of me, throw me over his shoulder, and then began heading back down the stairs."

Mr. Grimly paused again, and we became aware of the pain he must be experiencing by retelling the events of that horrific day. Taking another moment to compose himself, he continued, "Halfway down, the stairs collapsed in a burst of flames, and we fell to the first floor. My father and I were both caught on fire, and from what I remember, he wasn't moving. At that instant, my mother rushed in from the hallway entrance, grabbed hold of me, and dragged me out of the house. Her coat caught on fire, but she shrugged it off. I remember vividly the sound of fire engines and police sirens. The rescue team ran over to me and wrapped me in a blanket, putting out the fire. Unfortunately, my mother didn't listen to the fireman holding her, and escaping his grasp, she ran back into the burning house for my father.

"By that time, the paramedics had given me medicine that put me to sleep, so they could bandage me up. I didn't find out what happened until I woke up in the hospital the next day.

"Neither of my parents survived. My friend Walter did. He had a few scars, but eventually he fully recovered. Unfortunately for me, two-thirds of my body was burned, including most of my face. They did what they could at the time, but that was a long time ago, and they didn't have anything like what they have now for burn victims."

Pausing for a moment, he sadly concluded, "That's why I wear a mask because I don't want to frighten anyone."

With tears openly flowing down my face, I asked, "So that's why you only open your door on Halloween because it's OK to wear a mask then?"

Mr. Grimly replied slowly, "Yes, that's exactly why."

Then Addy asked, "And the reason you decorate your house during the night is so no one will see you?"

Mr. Grimly again replied, "Yes, that's true also."

Then, I hesitantly asked, "But why do you go through all that trouble on the holidays if you have no one to share it with?"

He replied unexpectedly with happiness filling his voice, "Well, you see, I love children very much. I had always wished to have a family, but as you can imagine, I never got a chance to meet someone special. So on holidays, I decorate the manor because children come from all over the town to see my creations. I get such pleasure from sneaking peeks at their shining, smiling faces, and that's where my joy comes from. It's knowing that I've made people happy in my own little way that brings me happiness."

I asked, "How can you possibly put everything up in one night—and no one has ever seen you do it?" Then thoughtfully, I asked, "Does someone help you?"

As I was sensing from his voice that he was actually smiling, Mr. Grimly replied, "Oh yes, I have help. You'd be surprised if I told you everything. But for now, let's just say that my old friend Walter comes by on occasion, and there's also a terrific fellow in the neighborhood who's been extremely helpful over the last several years."

"Mr. Grimly," I asked nervously, "I know you don't want to, but I'd really appreciate it if you would remove your mask." Quickly, I glanced at Skye and Addy, trying to gain a sense of approval. Intuitively, I felt a look of agreement.

Looking back toward Mr. Grimly, I continued, "We won't be frightened, we promise. It's just that not seeing you is much worse than anything we could imagine. Plus, we'd really like to see the real you."

Softly I continued, "Would you please do that for us? Would you remove your mask?"

He replied cautiously, "Are you absolutely sure?" We nodded our heads. Very slowly, he removed the mask and then raised his head looking at us. The first thing I saw was his beautiful blue eyes, filled with sorrow. His ears had been burned off, and there was hardly anything remaining of his nose or lips, but it didn't frighten me.

I glanced over at Addy to make sure she was handling it all right. I was completely astounded to hear Addy say cheerfully, "You're not half as scary as those masks!"

With relief, we all started laughing, including Mr. Grimly. Then I asked, "I'd love to come back with Fluffums and visit—maybe every week—BUT NO MASK! Is that all right?"

He was so happy when Skye and Addy asked if they could visit also. Without hesitation, he answered that he (and Puffin) would enjoy that more than anything in the world.

He replied, "You and your families will always be welcome at Grimly Manor. I haven't laughed since the day of the fire, and I owe it all to you three angels."

Skye replied, "Thanks, and by the way, not only do you have beautiful eyes, but you've also got the nicest set of teeth I've ever seen! So you just keep smiling!"

As we were getting ready to leave, one more thought occurred to me. I turned around and asked, "How do you keep your food cold without a refrigerator?"

"Oh!" He chuckled. "I have a root cellar, and I get ice delivered twice a week during the warm months. In the winter, it's cold enough down there to freeze a turkey!"

Skye then asked, "Well, how do you warm up your food without electricity or gas?"

Mr. Grimly smiled and replied, "Well there, Skye, I can either use my wood stove or my coal stove! By the way, how is it that you know I don't use any utilities?"

I answered, "Well, when you give us some more clues about how you decorate each holiday, then maybe we'll let you in on some of our secrets."

Mr. Grimly said, "In case you're curious, I don't use utilities because I live on a very small income, so I cut back where I can, and besides, I enjoy living the way my grandfathers did a hundred years ago. It's actually kind of fun! In case you're wondering, I have a well in the backyard where my water supply comes from. Are there any more utility questions?"

I replied, "No, not tonight, but maybe later, if you don't mind."

Mr. Grimly said, "You're welcome to ask, and by the way, Leira, your father and I have become good acquaintances."

I looked at him in total shock and bewilderment, then inquired hesitantly, "What exactly do you mean by that? You don't know my dad."

Mr. Grimly gave a somewhat sneaky smile and replied, while glancing at the three of us, "Did you really think your parents would allow you to accept gifts from a stranger or let you come in to thank me this evening?"

Skye, Addy, and I quickly looked at one another. I replied, "I suppose not, but we were so caught up in the mystery, I don't think we even thought about that."

Mr. Grimly responded, "That's what parents are for. They are there to watch over you and keep you safe. Oh, and by the way, I've been invited by each of your families for dinner next weekend! So I'll just have to decide where to go first!"

We were all laughing as we waved good-bye and set out homeward in what seemed to be another blizzard. Heads down, we braced ourselves for the storm. Holding hands, we trudged slowly back through the mounting drifts. Our faces felt like they were turning into icicles, but inside, our hearts were warm and cozy. We couldn't wait to cuddle up with our new puppies. The mystery of Grimly Manor was solved, and I hoped that sometime in the future we could have another great adventure to share!

I climbed into bed that night, with Fluffums asleep in her "waterproof pen" next to my bed. I lay awake for a little while, thinking about all the wonderful and exciting things that had happened over the last several months. I realized how very fortunate I was. As I drifted off to sleep, I imagined I heard the yipping of a puppy. I awoke slightly dazed and realized it wasn't a dream. Fluffums was standing up in her pen yipping noisily at me. I picked her up and placed her next to me. She climbed right above my head and curled herself around me. Then she fell soundly asleep! I felt like the luckiest girl in the whole world. I stayed awake for a short time, wondering what the next few months would bring. Little did I know that there was a serious adventure heading our way in February, during winter vacation!